CHATTER

Also by Perrin Ireland
Ana Imagined

CHATTER

A NOVEL BY PERRIN IRELAND

Algonquin Books of Chapel Hill | 2007

Published by
ALGONQUIN BOOKS OF CHAPEL HILL
Post Office Box 2225
Chapel Hill, North Carolina 27515-2225

a division of
Workman Publishing
225 Varick Street
New York, New York 10014

Lyrics on page 245 from "Spanish Pipedreams," words and
music by John Prine. Copyright © 1971 Walden Music, Inc. &
Sour Grapes Music. All rights on behalf of Walden Music, Inc.,
administered by WB Music Corp. All Rights Reserved.
Used by permission of Alfred Publishing Co., Inc.

This is a work of fiction. While, as in all fiction, the literary
perceptions and insights are based on experience, all names,
characters, places, and incidents either are products of the
author's imagination or are used fictitiously.

Library of Congress Cataloging-in-Publication Data
Ireland, Perrin.
Chatter: a novel / by Perrin Ireland.—1st ed.
p. cm.
ISBN-13: 978-1-56512-540-7
1. Marriage—Fiction. 2. Illegitimate children—Fiction.
I. Title.
PS3559.I82C47 2007
813'.6—dc22   2007006637

10 9 8 7 6 5 4 3 2 1
First Edition

for Tom,
without whom nothing is possible

for Sam,
who would prefer a Milk-Bone

for friends

Nothing is a long time ago.

AMY HEMPEL, *The Dog of the Marriage*

Acknowledgments

I will always be grateful to Leigh Feldman for her intelligence, warmth, professionalism, and humor. Also, to the indispensible Michelle Mortimer.

Thanks to Kathy Pories for her eye and passion for this material, which made it a better book, and to Bob Jones.

My enduring gratitude to a few of the many who've provided invaluable help along the way: Doug Bauer, Elizabeth Benedict, Sally Brady, Elizabeth Coxe, Margaret Drain, Meredith Friedman, Amy Hempel, Nancy Horn, Melinda Hurst, Sharon Kapp, Sheila Kohler, Rob Laubacher, Cynthia Linkas, Margot Livesey, Jill McCorkle, Askold Melnyczuk, Wanda Pedas, Joanne Pender, Liam Rector, Bob Shacochis, Patricia Straus, Tree Swenson, Leona Vogt, Laura Welsh, and, particularly, Betsy Seifter.

I thank family members who offered support, with *un grand embrazo* for nieces, nephews, and Scott Ramey.

Greatest thanks, always, to my beloved, long-suffering husband, Tom Ramey.

Before I met my husband, the strongest supporter of my writing was my mother, who trained to be a librarian, but raised three children instead.

Here.

American Found Dead Outside of Medellín

AP — WASHINGTON

Sources at the State Department report that the bullet-riddled body of a long-missing former Peace Corps volunteer, Eric Mariner, was found in the foothills of the Cordillera Central Mountains Saturday by members of a local militia. Mr. Mariner, originally from Teabrook, New Jersey, had completed two years in the Peace Corps in Latin America prior to his disappearance. An investigation into the cause of his death is under way.

If the article had appeared in Sarah's local newspaper, she would have criticized the "bullet-riddled" cliché.

She wouldn't have known it had anything to do with her.

PART ONE

Sarah could see half of her face in the mirror. She got dizzy when she thought about when you're looking at your right side in the mirror it's your left side.

She pressed her toes onto the cool white plastic scale, which was in Michael's bathroom.

On the shelf above the toilet, a scrap of paper stuck out from under shaving cream. Sarah moved the can of shaving cream and picked up the paper, which had been folded in half, and then half again. An odd hiding place.

Should she open it?

It was a message for Michael from one of those telephone answering pads. Camila Rodriguez had called, and the call was checked *Urgent*. Two days ago. Michael's secretary must have asked for the purpose of the call. "He'll know" was scrawled on the form.

This was not a name Sarah knew. She knew all of his business associates, all of his friends.

A Miami area code. Michael traveled frequently to Miami, often on his way to Latin America.

If Sarah mentioned the message to Michael, it would be considered evidence of snooping, a sin without equal. She tucked the note back under the can, which waited to eject its grinning white foam.

It was 6:30 p.m.

Al Qaeda had released a new video.

"IN THE SOAPS," Sarah said, "the husbands never go to work, preferring to stay at home to discuss relationships."

"I had to give a speech to the group from China," Michael said.

"And the husbands in the soaps rent entire restaurants, with bands, to celebrate their anniversaries."

"When I got back from the meeting, I had 243 e-mails." He tossed his briefcase on the floor, his jacket on the chocolate-stained antique chair. "How's Rachel?"

"I don't understand why my friends have cancer and the leader of North Korea doesn't." Sarah rose from the sofa, jeans bunched at the knee, and he followed her into the kitchen, where a microwave flashed the wrong time and splashes of water surrounded the dog dish.

"Why don't we get that thin pizza anymore?" he asked.

"There comes a point when you want a Dove Bar more than a roll in the hay."

"When did you start calling it a roll in the hay?"

"Norma saw you at lunch with someone who looked like the saleswoman from the Harley dealership."

"The new actuary."

"Here," she said. "Use my napkin. You spilled some on your shoe, too."

THEY'D BEEN MARRIED eighteen years, following divorces, and he had a daughter, Lisa, who'd lived with Sarah and Michael when she was a teenager; Sarah had no children of her own.

He was great-looking and mischievous and charming, particularly with company, and when she was younger, Sarah looked at least as good as other young women.

Their wooden house was old on the outside and new on the inside. One realtor called it Colonial, another identified it as Greek Revival — Sarah went with that.

SHE WIPED CONDENSATION from the windshield as the car in front of theirs loomed larger. The bumper sticker referred to unions, but the lettering was old and weak.

Michael drummed his fingers on the steering wheel; they had an agreement that he wouldn't drive more than fifteen miles an hour faster than the speed limit. He was in a hurry even though she was dragging him to the appointment.

Michael would be thinking about his numbers. Percentages, risk.

Sarah had a section in her closet for corporate wife clothes and another larger section for jeans and black. A jewelry box for demure earrings, another for dangling eccentrics.

The car accelerated, and suburban houses morphed into high-rises. They passed a flag at half-mast, a crumpled mass of blankets. Yesterday Sarah had seen a program about children who'd lost limbs to land mines; the possibility of being a force for good in the world seemed remote.

In the backseat, Random, the beagle, ripped into a piece of Kleenex. A bottle of water — still, not sparkling — rolled across the floor, and candy wrappers filled the trash receptacle. Michael chewed gum, which he promised to dispense with before they met someone who mattered.

"I was thinking of writing a different kind of novel," Sarah said. "About a married couple."

"What's the plot?"

"Someone's a murderer."

"Did you see that Ferrari back there? The red one? It's the new model."

They passed a newsstand. "Terrorist Chatter Up."

• • •

SARAH STRAIGHTENED THE frame of the terrible poem on the waiting room wall. Her relationship to poetry was tenuous but deeply felt. She planned to read ten poems a day, to stay smart, but didn't.

Michael flipped through *Psychology Today,* bouncing his leg until the chair shook, and paused at an article about runner's high.

A tree with bright purple blossoms startled at the window.

An elderly woman entered, tugging a small girl. A warm grandmother could save a girl's life, Sarah had learned that from a psychologist friend. All it takes is one good person. Sarah had known none of her grandparents. Michael's grandfather, head of the household during the frequent occasions when Michael's father was overseas, had been alcoholic.

Michael held the magazine in front of his face.

"Hello," Sarah said.

SHE PRECEDED MICHAEL into the counselor's office, where they'd been coming for two months, and sat in her chair. "We've been getting along fairly well since last time."

Michael scratched his left calf. He had runner's calves and slender ankles.

"More positive," Sarah said. "He's less likely to fly off

the handle." She brushed a hair off her jeans, and wondered where the expression came from, *fly off the handle*. Her hard chair was the low, scooped-out plastic kind that used to look space-agey and now looked dated. The white noise machine hummed happily outside the door, and the rug, which was geometric rather than floral, smelled of wet wool.

The things she wanted to say she couldn't.

Sometimes she was hard on Michael, she was learning, which was a shock to her. What he was learning was a mystery.

A photograph of two men with their arms linked sat on the desk.

"A few days ago he told me I looked good," Sarah said. "It felt a little like handsome, but still . . ."

Michael wore a maroon tie; most of his ties were maroon, because they go with white shirts and suits that are blue, black, gray, or brown. Today was gray.

"We're not the sort of married people who don't talk to each other at restaurants," Michael said.

"He writes wonderful letters when we're apart," Sarah said. "I don't understand the discrepancy between what he says to me and what he writes to me." She glanced at the shelves; all the books were about diving. "Michael refuses to discuss parts of his past."

An anxious-looking window washer peered in from scaffolding.

"WILL YOU BE TURNING out the light soon?" Michael slid *Bikers' World* to the floor by the bed and turned on the television. Sarah hadn't told him that middle-aged men look silly on motorcycles, sirens screaming MIDLIFE CRISIS!

"Soon," Sarah said, scribbling notes on the last page of the paperback she was reading, *Why Did I Ever.*

Michael flipped to the weather. The TV sat on an airy, Plexiglas stand, and wasn't hidden the way their neigh-bors' was mind.

"I don't know when I've felt so hopeless," Sarah said, wearing a wrinkled Formaggio T-shirt.

"Partly sunny tomorrow," Michael said.

"I was thinking of calling the husband Cooper, and the wife's name is Susannah, or Whitney."

"What are you titling it?"

"Susannah and Cooper."

"You usually have more interesting titles."

"I'm hoping someone will think it's a romance and buy it by mistake." Sarah's dwindling interest in romance concerned her, although she did like sentimental televi-sion movies about princesses and movie stars.

"Did you like Ed's jacket?" Michael asked, turning the clock to face the wall. "I like the old aviator jackets." His hair whirled in the back from slouching in his chair.

"I once loved a man for the cracks in his leather jacket," Sarah said. "Do you think they should have a dog? Maybe a small one." She scratched out a sentence. "I got tickets for the Soweto Gospel Choir tomorrow night." Politics, God, and art were three of her favorite things, and music was king of the arts, although she couldn't make it herself. Sometimes when musicians played together it was sexier than sex.

"I go to New York tomorrow," Michael said.

"The husband's having an affair," Sarah said.

IF HE IS HAVING an affair, I'm cutting out the crotches of his suits, unless that's a cliché, and I believe it is. Sarah slipped her feet into the steel stirrups.

"Don't worry," the gynecologist said. "I didn't have time to shave my legs either. Scoot closer." Her blonde curls drizzled over black eyes.

A rack of pamphlets about battered women and sexual abuse hung next to the door beside a notice announcing that you should ask your doctor if she's washed her hands. Sticks with cotton at the end stuck out of a glass jar on the counter.

Sarah wanted to feel safe. She got physically ill when Michael was out of town — fever, nausea, fatigue, trembling, breathlessness. She felt faint. And got well the second he returned. The doctor's window faced the parking lot. Were there men with binoculars?

"Relax," the doctor said.

The smudge on the ceiling looked like Mount Fuji.

"Now you'll feel the speculum."

She got Fuji and Kilimanjaro mixed up.

"The clamp."

"How's your baby?" Sarah asked. The woman's breasts, near to overflowing, pushed against her blouse.

"I'm not getting any sleep," the doctor said.

"I tried Benadryl," Sarah said.

"Now the pap smear."

Melatonin never worked.

"I'll do the manual exam. You'll feel pressure."

Pressure. Michael had had affairs in his previous marriage, although his wife went first, he said. Sarah's mother had had an affair. Was it, or was it not, justifiable?

Pressure. And Sarah's first husband had had affairs. Before that, she had a fiancé killed in Vietnam, but this was not the sort of list you could put in a novel, for example, to indicate why a character had certain fears. Overkill.

SARAH PICKED UP the phone and listened for a dial tone, but it seemed to be working. Michael had usually called by now. Eight hours since he left for New York. She couldn't find the slip of paper with the name of his hotel.

If she had a real job, she wouldn't be obsessing about Michael, and she wouldn't be obsessing about Michael if he hadn't been unusually evasive. He was always evasive when there was something important that he didn't want her to know, something she wouldn't be happy knowing, but he'd never been *this* secretive, *this* nervous. She replaced the receiver and reached for the frayed red leash. Random ran in circles.

The door slammed behind them, and Sarah marched purposefully toward the park, past pale spring leaves like Baby Bibb lettuce, past a flag at half-mast. She crossed the street to avoid the large boxer, and Random circled her and lunged forward before Sarah turned and unwound herself. A pedestrian approached, and Sarah moved to the right of the sidewalk, but the man continued to hug the same side, so Sarah stepped to the left just as he moved in the same direction. She stopped, and let him pass.

At the traffic light she pivoted, blocks short of the park, and returned to the house; she picked up the phone and listened for a dial tone.

THE GAP SELLS BRAS — who knew. Sarah followed twenty-four-year-old Lisa, Michael's daughter, on her serpentine trek through counters and racks, as bright overhead lights illuminated the size-two students who populate Harvard Square. Forget buying a bathing suit here.

Lisa checked the size of a black T-shirt, the trace of a sesame noodle shiny on her lime green spaghetti-strap blouse. Her black lace-up boots opened untied at the top, and a short, sprightly ponytail sprang from the crown of her head, the kind five-year-olds wore in Sarah's day. Last Christmas Sarah had given Lisa clothes that Sarah considered appropriate; it was one of the few times Lisa had become enraged with her.

"Have you heard from your father since he left on his trip?" Sarah asked, ten hours after his departure. Michael called while waiting for planes and room service.

"Where is he this time?" Lisa asked.

Multicolored tank tops hung next to striped and dotted bikini underpants (high cut), and mittens and scarves decorated a far wall. The sales clerks were also young and thin.

Women holding clothes lined up for fitting rooms. "She said all the adulterers in the room should stand up," one said to another.

"My mother's having a hard time again," Lisa said. "One crying jag after another."

"Sorry . . ." Sarah said, bumping into another shopper.

"Cries and cries . . ." Lisa said. "She says if I went back to live with her, that would help."

Racks of jeans stood at attention like armies.

THE BABY BLUE Virgin Mary watched as Sarah hurried, late, across the lawn to Michael's boyhood home, just twenty minutes from Boston. It was uphill, across freshly cut grass, the sweet smell of it reaching the porch of the small, steep-roofed wooden house. When Michael was out of town, Sarah filled her days with appointments, this time with overdue visits to relatives.

Paul, Michael's father, opened the door, as Marie, Michael's mother, craned her neck to see from the living room; Sarah hugged Paul, lingering on the navy blue velour shirt. He was bald in front, with a mustache that was whiter than the hair on his head.

"Where is he this time?" he asked. "Why don't you go with him?"

On a shelf, a photograph of seven-year-old Michael wearing an Indian headdress. *An only child is a lonely child* — was that true? A picture of Lisa with her mother and a younger Michael on a sailboat.

"Come sit by me, hon." Marie patted the flowered sofa. Her henna hair looked mistaken.

A Dean's Auto Parts pen rolled across the coffee table; Paul had worked in the auto repair business after retiring as a sergeant in the army. A ragged recipe had been torn out of a magazine.

"Hungry?" Marie asked, as Sarah sat down.

"I had several tablespoons of peanut butter before I came."

Marie reached over to pinch Sarah's cheek. "Like a bird." She leaned back against the sofa. "Lisa's mother is having a hard time again. Cries and cries . . . She thinks we should spend Christmas together."

Paul punched a CD into a player, and Frank Sinatra

began to sing. Paul bowed and extended a dancing hand to Sarah, his tummy pouring over his belt.

"I don't remember how," she said, sliding her feet under the sofa.

"I do."

"Was Sinatra mafia?" she asked.

"We have eggplant parmesan," Marie said. She was thin, with eyebrows frozen in surprise.

"Did your ancestors own slaves?" Paul asked Sarah.

Sarah had been afraid to research the slave issue, but one day stumbled on a newspaper clipping about her great-great-grandmother's death, when she'd been surrounded by the former slaves who'd been *so* fond of her, according to the Mississippi paper.

When Sarah's southern high school was integrated, she sat quietly as the new students were taunted, reluctant to jeopardize her own newcomer status.

Paul and Marie's kitchen was splashed with brightly colored pot holders, dish towels, and ceramic figures. The raccoon-eyed cat curled, sleeping, in the corner, and pictures of young children covered the refrigerator door.

"For you," Marie said, handing Sarah *The Joy of Cooking,* and sitting at the kitchen table.

"Michael likes Cheerios," Sarah said.

"Look at this," Marie said, indicating a large tan corrugated cardboard box on the table. "I've been in the attic." She plucked a partially used roll of Scotch tape out of the box. "Michael gave this to me when he was in kindergarten — my Christmas present." Setting the tape down, she pulled out a squashed box of Kleenex. "This was my birthday present. He earned twenty-five cents for cleaning out old Mr. Costello's ears next door.

"When Michael got that job in Washington, he made the down payment on our first house," Marie said, settling into the chair. "*I* would have hired him for that job. I would have hired him for any job."

"You've got to see these guys!" Paul banged into the room. "The Sox are pulling it off!" He opened the refrigerator and removed a plate of half-eaten Cornish hen, the old icebox shuddering when he slammed the door.

Water dripped from the faucet at thirty-second intervals. Clutching the tape, Sarah followed Paul and Marie into the living room.

DISTANT THUNDER CONTRADICTED afternoon sun pouring through Sarah's parents' window. She sat on the chintz sofa as her father passed her a silver tray with a glass of water on a thin, white linen cocktail napkin, and her mother crossed her legs under the teal dress, stroking the arm of the wing chair.

"Michael's traveling more than usual," her mother said, shifting her emery board from one hand to the other. The Anne Tyler book she was reading — smart but not obscure — lay on the end table.

"The number of crises is exploding," Sarah said.

"There have always been crises," her mother said. When her mother was a child and her dog had been run over by a car she was required to take her piano lesson anyway.

"He's gotten the tickets for *Lion King*," Sarah said.

"Tell me again why we have to see that?" A pearl-encrusted Bible sitting on the shelf behind her.

Sarah ran her finger along an antique vase, the crack repaired. A large photograph of Sarah as a chubby, happy child sat on a table, her brother standing serious and older behind her.

"Is everything alright?" her mother asked.

"Michael will come home," her father said, picking up *Foreign Affairs*. Her father's mother had once been a missionary in China, and, at meals, he and his siblings were required to recite a Bible verse; there was always a great rush to be the first to say "Jesus wept," the shortest verse in the Bible, and he could still sing "Jesus Loves Me" in Chinese.

"What are you calling your book?" her mother asked. She'd been to the beauty parlor, and the wave at her forehead was firmly in place.

"Whitney and Cooper."

"You usually have more interesting titles."

"You wouldn't buy a book titled 'Whitney and Cooper'?"

Her mother leaned back in her chair. "What's on the cover?"

"Maybe two hands not quite reaching each other."

"Like the Sistine Chapel?"

"Oh." Out the window, the Chinese garden table stood on the patio. "That poet — which one was it — said originality is just a fresh amalgam of influences."

Her mother massaged her temple. "You give him too much leash."

Sarah studied the oil painting of her great-grandmother above the mantel. She was plain, plain.

"I remember the surprise birthday party Michael had for you when you were engaged," her mother said. "That was lovely."

"He said I was an exciting woman." Sarah looked out the window. "I was working then." Her father had bought the Chinese garden table on a trip. Once he'd sent her a postcard from Australia: "These kangaroos have almost as much bounce in their step as you and Mommie."

Sarah rose and headed for the door. She stopped and looked around the room. "Did you change something?"

"No," her mother said.

THE TOXIC LIQUID dripped from the IV into Rachel's vein, as Sarah tried to concentrate on her friend's heart-shaped face, the blue-black hair. Their chemotherapy booth was cozy — two chairs, a TV, magazines, a window overlooking people fighting for parking spaces on the street below.

Rachel reclined in the armchair as if she were on the deck of a cruise ship. "I have three new clients," she said. "I can't tell them I'm sick."

"Could you be just a little sick?"

"Not with new clients."

Sarah felt a stab of pain in what she assumed was her ovary. The seat of the chair was too deep and her neck hurt as she twisted to face Rachel, the walls of the cubicle too close to turn the large chairs toward each other. A print of sunflowers hung above Rachel.

"I like your cross," Rachel said. "It's tiny, discreet   "

"Thank you," Sarah said, putting her hand to her throat, letting the metal slip back behind her collar. The sweater over her blouse hid wrinkles.

A nurse pushed her head in, then pulled the short flowered curtains shut again, a gesture of privacy. A roach scurried across the floor, and Sarah stood and walked toward it.

"What are you doing?" Rachel asked.

"Stretching my legs." Sarah slammed her foot down, but missed.

Rachel picked up a copy of *Newsweek* and threw it at the roach, which crawled out from under it and into a crack in the wall. "*Architectural Digest* would have done it," she said. She wore a beige suit with green earrings, peridot, about which Sarah had just learned. Sarah wore baggy black pants with an elastic waistband, and her watch was silver but far enough away from the gold necklace to be okay.

She returned to her seat, and tapped her fingers on the arm of the chair.

"Where is he this time?" Rachel asked. "Why don't you go with him?"

"Our American Express bill included an item from a Hallmark store," Sarah said.

"That can't be for you." Rachel shifted in her seat. "Did you see him with Antonia the other night? I could never be married to someone so extroverted."

There's no harm in flirting, Michael would say. Except to your wife, and the person you're leading on. Once when they were bored at a dinner party, she and Michael pretended they'd just met; she was stunned by his skill. The ready smile, the quick wit, the wink, the energizing surge of testosterone.

Rachel caught herself. "He's a wonderful man, and it's great the way he supported you when you went to graduate school." She scrutinized the collar of Sarah's blouse. "That's not your color, is it?"

It wasn't. Sarah slumped a little with the knowledge of looking wan.

With her free hand, Rachel poked around in her backpack and handed Sarah a book of Vietnamese poetry. "My neighbor's a reviewer — I found it in his trash."

Sarah fondled the book, turning it slowly from side to side, then opened it and slid a finger tenderly down the length of a poem, trying to remember the first poem she'd loved. *Only God can make a tree?*

She looked up at the bag of chemicals hanging from the steel hook, the plastic bag squished at the top. "What's your fantasy trip?" She didn't look at the needle penetrating Rachel's arm.

"The Galápagos."

"Turtles?"

"The most extraordinary birds."

Once she and Rachel had spent a weekend at Truro. The light, the dunes. Enchanted moonscape. Rachel had given Sarah a lecture about being paranoid.

A car horn.

"I have a question!" Rachel shouted to a passing doctor's legs.

He parted the curtains.

"This Ativan I'm taking, to sleep," Rachel said. "Is it addictive? Am I going to have trouble getting off of it when I recover?"

Everything was in slow motion, under water, the doctor's mouth moving, the words swimming across the room.

"IT'S SILLY OF ME," Sarah said to Michael's secretary, switching the telephone receiver from one ear to the other. "I always put the name of his hotel right by the phone."

Not that I ever call him, I mean I rarely *call him, as you know, because I know how busy he is — you all have so much to do, I know that, not that you do everything together, but just whatever is the appropriate number of things, it makes sense that he gets your colds, viruses are transmitted primarily by hand — the papers passing back and forth . . .*

ALTHOUGH MICHAEL'S SECRETARY had given her the number of the hotel, some things are better than calling. Sarah had never done this before.

She pulled the black suitcase out of the closet, and Random began to whimper; he crawled to a corner of the bedroom and lay down and watched as she tossed a variety of black items into the bag, along with vitamins, toothpaste, Kleenex. He stood at attention.

Paintings (abstract females) and photographs covered the walls of the room, where sweaters and blouses hung over the backs of chairs. Shoes tumbled at odd angles, some paired, some not, on the floor of the open closet, and Coetzee and the *Boston Globe* lay on the unmade bed. Michael's reading glasses perched on a book about Lewis and Clark; she loved that he read, so many husbands didn't. He accepted book recommendations from her and would read fiction if he could learn something.

In the bathroom, liquid soap waited on the counter next to the Benadryl and shampoo. When they were dating, Michael whistled in the shower, and when they were dating, she cooked, except the night the United States bombed Libya. *I don't cook during wars,* she'd said.

Sometimes Sarah and Michael had marital fireworks, both the good and the bad kind. Other times, they could go for days immersing themselves in life's details in silent, mutual recognition that they were neither pleased nor displeased with one another, respectful of indifference, tolerant of gray, as they marked the time awaiting what came always, and always unannounced — the suddenness of passion.

THE CAB DRIVER clicked the doors shut and looked back at the house as he pulled away on their recovering-from-winter road, potholes distributed like an obstacle course.

Why were some bald heads shiny and others dull? It was one of those cabs with a cage wall between the front and back seats, and they took a corner on what felt like two wheels, as a copy of the *Herald* slid down the seat toward Sarah. Another turn, on other wheels. Cookie crumbs were pressed into the floor.

"Are you a teacher?" the driver asked. People in Boston were asked that.

"A writer." They passed the mansard with the Samoyed.

"Books?"

"When they let me." A bus advertising a reality TV

show chugged along beside them, and a cyclist weaved between cars.

"Thick books?"

"Slim."

"Ran out of things to say?"

"Said them quickly."

Sarah opened her compact to check her lipstick, which had spread to her teeth and chin. Lisa would be giving Random the foods he was forbidden to eat. She liked staying at the house while they were gone. Were there parties, and were the men nice. Sometimes Sarah worried that Lisa hadn't found a steady boyfriend. Other times, immense relief.

"Where are you from?" the driver asked.

"Virginia, originally." Smokers huddled at the entrance to an office building. "I worked in Washington for years."

Vietnam, Watergate, inaugurations, State of the Union messages. The Hawk 'n' Dove Restaurant, picnics at Theodore Roosevelt Island, weekends at Rehoboth Beach, the National-Best-Frickin'-Gallery-of-Art in the world.

The night, after the bourbon, when they decided to jump into every fountain in the city. The apartment where Michael had said, *I want to spend the rest of my life with you.* Where he had told her she should wear tighter clothes so people could see, and then said, *Is it okay to say that?*

"I've been South," the driver said. "I was in New Orleans once. Went to this club, they had these dancers, and some really good-looking men dancers, only it turned out the men were actually women, dressed as guys. Unbelievable, you would never have guessed it, like it was a joke on us."

He watched Sarah in the rearview mirror. "I went back to her dressing room afterwards, the dressing room of the most beautiful one. I took off her clothes, the man clothes, and made her perform as a woman."

He put a beefy arm on the back of the seat and turned around to look at Sarah. "Do you understand?" He leaned toward her, his eyes boring into hers. "I made her perform as a woman."

"This is close enough," Sarah said.

GUM HAD ADHERED to the bottom of Sarah's shoe, and she kicked it off in the train station high as a cathedral. She wished Michael were there, an umbrella for worries.

She pushed and pulled her rolling suitcase into the luggage compartment at the head of the rail car, and moved down the aisle in search of two adjacent empty seats. She took the aisle seat, dropping her black tote bag onto the adjoining seat, and looked at both ends of the car to locate the restroom and the café, then pulled out her book.

"Is that seat taken?" He was middle-aged, also, in a wrinkled, too hot, tweed jacket and jeans, pleasant enough, with tousled, flyaway hair over the rimless glasses. She could kill him.

Stepping on her foot and slapping her face with his battered leather briefcase, he climbed across to the window seat. "Going to New York?" he asked. Dark mixed with a little gray in his beard, and he wore what were called work boots in the sixties.

"To find — meet — my husband." An Amtrak magazine with glossy pictures of places it would be fun to visit was stuck in the back pocket of the seat in front of her. The footrest raised so there was room for her bag on the dirty floor.

"My wife's work is being exhibited in a new gallery," he said. "And then I have a meeting." His shoelaces had missed some holes.

"What kind of art?"

"She's doing a series of close-ups of triangles, from different perspectives." His face dropped into his hands. "I hate it."

"I'm sure it's admired by the right people," she said.

"I'm going for coffee," he said.

He was lanky, and zigzagged down the aisle as the train twisted and turned with the bounce in his step that Sarah equated with healthy testosterone levels; she knew eighty-year-old men who had it, such an attractive quality. He pressed the spot that opened the door between cars, and disappeared as a mother and two children streamed into view.

Low-cost housing faded into scraggly fields which evolved into green meadows. Telephone poles and wires, the curve of tracks ahead. A river, but no regular person would say "runs through."

He'd pulled John Ashbery out of his briefcase, but the book lay unread on his lap. He spoke in admiring terms of the Charles, and she said it looked like a creek compared to the Potomac. He asked if she was from Washington.

"My father was in the foreign service. Thirteen."

"Thirteen?"

"That's how many schools I went to, that's the next question, and then you'll ask how I liked moving around, I hated it. Did you come to Boston to go to school and stay because you liked it?"

He had turned to face her. "I came to Boston because of a job and stayed because my wife won't leave her shrink." The white "napkin" behind his head had flown over the top of the seat.

"What's so great about her shrink?"

"She teaches at Harvard and wears stylish clothes. She's the kind of person my wife would like to have as a friend. Or be."

Sarah was between shrinks; she had Rachel. Therapists fill the void created by the absence of a good relationship, a therapist had told her.

A woman walking down the aisle was jolted into Sarah's lap, and removed herself, apologizing profusely. She wore a dress and heels, and it looked as if there should be seams on her stockings.

Sarah's seatmate — Jacob was his name — tipped his

Styrofoam coffee into his mouth. The bathroom door was ajar, and clanged shut whenever the train made a turn, and then slid open again. A trickle of water snaked across the floor, and odor emerged. The girl in front of Sarah, visible in the crevice between seats, stared out at the rushing landscape, while across the aisle, someone slept.

"What job?" Sarah asked Jacob.

"What?"

"Brought you to Boston."

"I head up a nonprofit, medical research, trying to find ways to bring health care to people who don't have access." He seemed bored with his explanation, as she'd been when she'd had a job too long.

"Interesting that you said you head up an organization, instead of that you work for one."

"I'm a guy." With irritation?

"I bet you have pictures in your office of yourself in various interesting settings and costumes."

"There's one on my boat, but my son's at the helm. The safari picture was taken by someone else, I didn't even know it was happening."

"Men have pictures of themselves; women have pictures of people they love." Sarah had pictures of Michael from their early days together, pictures of her women friends, and Random in recent years.

"I have a picture of my wife."

"Because she asked you to," Sarah said. "Does your wife understand you?"

"I'm afraid so."

"So, if you were to get involved with someone else, it would be based on attraction, not on any lack in your marriage," she said. A research opportunity.

Toward the end of their marriage, Sarah and her first husband had separated for a week (her idea), with permission to sleep with others. After the first night, Sarah had satisfied her curiosity about her new lover, and spent the rest of the week in agony imagining her husband's activities. When they got back together, he admired her breasts, which he'd never noticed.

If you'd been married before, you knew that certain traits were *male* characteristics, and shouldn't be interpreted as repugnant idiosyncracies of your current spouse.

"Does your husband neglect you?" Jacob asked, glancing out the window. He looked at his watch.

"Not as much as he might," she said. "*Neglect*'s an interesting word, I could name a dog, or a book, that, although I've always thought *Lament* the most beautiful name. Doesn't *lament* conjure up a whole story?"

"I always thought *conjure* itself a beautiful word."

"I heard the director of the FBI on television yesterday," she said, "referring to a 'Terror Matrix.' That could be a title but I wouldn't buy it."

He looked at his watch again.

A smokestack flew past. After September 11, Michael had given her an engagement ring, the kind they couldn't afford when they got married. *Because of all it made me think.*

"Homeland Security says Internet chatter is up," Sarah said, fingering a bag of M&M's in her purse.

"Where were you when it happened?" he asked.

"Alone."

"We all were."

He had the kind of dark eyes that some writers would relate to pools. She lowered her gaze.

SARAH'S SHOULDERS PRESSED into the backseat of the taxi. Buildings raced past, so tall they seemed to bend over the cab, as if they might collapse onto it. The smell of sidewalk pretzels.

"See that man over there?" the driver said. "He's at that corner every afternoon, at 3:30, holding an amaryllis — do you know that flower?"

The man wore a suit and tie and had a neatly trimmed mustache. No evidence of impatience.

"It's odd," she said. "I like that."

The first night newly divorced Michael had come to her apartment for dinner, he'd brought flowers *and* wine, uncertain which was the appropriate offering, and she'd cooked a casserole, giving the leftovers to her date the next night, but soon she and Michael had caucused and negotiated an exclusive agreement. *I'm not doing this unilaterally,* she'd stated. They were Washingtonians.

"The rain this morning," the driver said. "I had enough rain thirty-five years ago to last a lifetime."

The picture on his permit was of a dark man, heavy-lidded. He looked old.

Thirty-five years would be Vietnam, her age.

In 1968, Sarah's five-year-old nephew wore a University of Virginia T-shirt, and she didn't have the heart to pass on her certain knowledge that the planet would no longer exist when he was old enough to go to college.

"I was in Chicago a couple of months ago," the driver said, "picking up one of my buddies — one of the guys from our platoon called and said he'd seen him on the streets — and I brought him back here, to the VA hospital." They moved through a sea of blaring horns, geese gone mad. "I talk to his mother on the phone all the time now. It's like she's *my* mom."

The taxi came to a stop in front of the hotel.

Michael used to stay at the Marriott World Trade Center. They would stay there together when she had work in New York; Michael would schedule meetings to coincide with hers. They'd come to New York on their honeymoon, both to work.

What was the proper relationship with a doorman? Sarah waited until the hotel's revolving door had turned several times before entering, the way, as a child, she'd stepped into the double jump ropes at precisely the right juncture, having memorized the rhythm.

The polished marble floor that rose to meet her was

sliced through by a green carpet bordered with gold leading to the reception desk. A long line blocked her path,
and Sarah proceeded toward its end, behind a young man
in a dark suit with dandruff on his left shoulder. The heels
on his expensive shoes were worn, and Sarah decided
he had a wife and two children in Michigan whom he
treated with tolerance between affairs. The man turned
around, revealing his clerical collar.

The line wasn't moving. A man behind her made a
noise that could be throat-clearing or "Achtung!"

The café opened to the left of the lobby.

"WILL SOMEONE BE joining you?" the maître d' asked as
Sarah looked to see if there was a table near the window.

Opening the menu at her table by the kitchen, Sarah
studied piles of arugula, crab bisque, risotto. Sandwiches
were called the Donald Trump, the Al Pacino. The best
actor in the world.

Heavy, garlicky smells rolled out of the kitchen, where
the chatter was loud and foreign, and the swinging door
was busy. A group of waiters surrounded a table singing
happy birthday in Spanish, and a balding man with a
bow tie, who might have followed her down from Boston, picked over his veal, decidedly uninterested in his
companion's conversation. Two women leaned across a
table toward each other, hungry for the intimacy their

confessions delivered, and Glenn Close sat at a table by the window with someone who wasn't a movie star.

That looks like the back of Michael's head. *Isn't it odd how we think we see people we know everywhere, particularly in New York.*

He turned toward the window, and it *was* Michael, sitting across from an attractive, dark-haired woman who looked to be around thirty. *Dear God. A Latina. Of course.* Sarah tried to catch her heart, she meant *breath.*

There would be an explanation.

People in the restaurant turned wavy, woozy.

Sarah's thirteen-year-old waiter appeared.

"I have to make a phone call," Sarah said, rising. Her upper and lower teeth were clicking against each other in odd configurations, and she couldn't remember how to fit them together naturally, as she pushed her way into the lobby.

She would. Make a phone call. To Jacob, from the train. He'd asked her to call if she had any time to kill. They could have coffee, he'd said, if she had nothing better to do. Looking out the window, coughing.

Dragging leaden limbs across the lobby, Sarah weaved between members of a rock band, and pulled the piece of paper with the number of Jacob's hotel from her pocket.

"This is Sarah," she said when she heard his voice. "I spilled Maalox on your notarized documents."

• • •

PLACING THE RECEIVER back on its hook, she turned and bumped into a wife-type person behind her. "I'm sorry..."

Now, however, she would have the courage to face Michael. She was loved. Or at least good enough for coffee. She tightened her belt and wet her lips before entering the café, and proceeded to their table, waiting for Michael, wearing a tie she'd given him, to notice her.

He jumped up. "Sarah . . ." He moved to embrace her, but Sarah retreated, watching the attractive young woman at the table, who eyed her with curiosity. The eyes were unusually blue for an olive-skinned brunette, and she wore tight jeans over her boots and a sky blue chenille top. Her wavy, shoulder-length, dark hair was too long, but when you look like that, you don't have to be chic.

"This is Camila..." Michael said. "My daughter."

THE COOL WASHCLOTH rested on Sarah's forehead as she lay on the hotel bed. She picked up the white cloth, examined it, and dropped it down on its other side like a flapjack, a piece of horsehair stitching from the bed's flowery comforter jabbing her in the back.

Camila had caught a flight back to Miami to meet a deadline; she was a journalist. She'd accomplished her goal, at least her initial goal, having had two meetings with Michael, whom she'd located on the Internet. She hadn't revealed much about herself, Michael said, mostly pummeling him with questions about his childhood and family. His/her origins.

She'd been decidedly unhappy about Sarah's arrival. Had she been the one to persuade Michael to keep their meeting secret?

This family is overflowing with daughters, none of them mine.

Before they were married, Sarah and Michael had gone to a psychic, and Sarah, who'd been thirty-eight, asked the man if she should have a baby. *Not now,* he'd said with disgust.

That wasn't the only reason; there was the bigger one. And then, soon, it was too late.

Once in a grocery store checkout line, Sarah had come close to grabbing a baby held by the woman in front of her and running out the door.

Michael sat on a chair by the Queen Anne desk, head in his hands. "I didn't know Camila existed until recently."

It must have been a brief affair, meaningless.

Picking up a pen from the desk, he doodled on a pad of paper. "When I was in the Peace Corps . . ."

He'd always been amnesiac about his Peace Corps years.

He put the pen down and stood.

"There was this woman . . ."

"Was it a one-night stand?" Sarah asked.

He paced, ending up by the door where he leaned his head against the evacuation plan. "I don't know why I should have to talk about Magdalena." He stood. "Tell me again why you're in New York."

"Research on the post-9/11 milieu, for my book, spur of the moment." The truth could bring on divorce.

Michael was not the sort of person who could be pushed, and he would tell the story at his own pace. A contrarian. Too many childhood battles for control lost to his grandfather.

He hated dwelling on the past. Michael had one gear — forward.

SARAH STEPPED OVER a dried-up contact lens in the sidewalk, marveling that she'd been able to wear heels to work all those years. Michael walked beside her, a little ahead, Manhattan rush-hour traffic throbbing around them.

"Keep going," she said. She had a mission — to determine what kind of threat Magdalena represented or, more probably, Camila, because everyone knew that the primary reason second marriages fail was because of children from previous relationships. *If we were on a sinking boat, who would you save?* The line of people needing rescue was lengthening.

Michael had a friend who'd found out he had a grown son from Vietnam, and first he met with the son, then the son's mother, before leaving his wife and moving in with the mother. If his wife had had children, it might have been different.

Sarah would start at the beginning, with Magdalena, and work up to Camila.

"Magdalena was the daughter of the biggest rancher in the area," Michael said. "She was nineteen, used to hang out with the Peace Corps volunteers, kind of a sidekick." They forced their way through stalled cars at an intersection, horns grating, Sarah struggling to keep up. The sidewalk thick with pedestrians bobbing and weaving, the colors and shapes dizzying, the women six-foot models.

"She was hungry for all things American," Michael said, "and used to read all our books." He turned to her. "Volunteers were each issued a footlocker full."

A drop of water fell from an air conditioner several stories above them, and Sarah changed course to avoid a repeat. "What did you read?"

"Steinbeck, Hemingway, Kerouac."

"And how did Magdalena find Kerouac?"

"She liked someone named Jean Rhys that the female volunteers were reading."

"She spoke English."

"Of course. She was educated, cosmopolitan."

An antique Buick sat at the curb, as if they were in Cuba. Before they met, Michael had been to Cuba on a sailboat during the most interesting chapter of his life, before he began devoting himself to business, worrying,

worrying. All the people whose jobs and families depended on his not screwing up.

"What was the Peace Corps doing there?" she asked.

"Most people in that part of the country were unspeakably poor — it was rural, campesinos."

"What did you do for them?"

"Community development."

"What did you *do*?"

"Dug ditches and put in pipe, for water."

"They were grateful?"

"Distracted."

"Not grateful?"

"I think they were grateful. After we put in the last piece of pipe, everyone got drunk."

"Tell me again why you joined the Peace Corps."

"Kennedy. I put on a blue and white seersucker suit, picked up a patched, brown leather suitcase, and got on a jet because of John Fitzgerald Kennedy. Armies of us."

"Some of us were content to check out the poetry of Robert Frost."

"He was a nasty man, you know, Frost."

"What does Magdalena mean?"

"Magdalena."

"Not 'fragrant flower' or 'gentle river'?"

"She invited a bunch of us over to her father's ranch one day for an *asado,* a kind of barbecue, and we spent the afternoon horseback riding, swimming in the river, that sort of thing."

Sarah moved behind him to sidestep a puddle. He had the best ass in the Western hemisphere.

He looked at his watch. "My meeting's at 10:30."

"What is it?"

"The Russian thing."

"Good luck."

"I have a date!" she said suddenly.

"A date?"

"Well it was a date, when I thought you were being unfaithful.

"Am I allowed to date? Who is this guy?"

"He's short."

"Do what you want."

SARAH WRAPPED HER LEG around the black wrought-iron chair at the outdoor café, and Jacob draped his jacket over the back of a chair. "I don't think of myself as short," he said.

"Does anyone think of himself as short?" she said. "Did Napoleon think of himself as short?"

"I suppose Josephine did. Why are we having this conversation?" He waved away the premature waiter, and placed his Frank Bidart book on the table; Sarah felt tingly.

A pigeon edged toward his chair. A child at another table cried. Sarah had seen a father with a small child in a grocery store last week, and the father had asked the girl whether they should select a red or yellow basket for their groceries. Sarah drew a breath. That would have been nice. If she'd had a child, there would have been choices about clothes and earrings and makeup, but not about homework and bedtime and saying yes ma'am and sir even if they didn't live in the South anymore.

"I'm afraid my novel might turn into a romantic comedy."

"What do you want it to turn into?"

"I would love to create something grand and glorious in the service of God the way Bach did, but I cannot, for the life of me, figure out how." When she was secure about the rest — Michael, food, water — this was Sarah's wrestle, how to be a force for good. Was there a chance that writing could qualify. Time running out.

Jacob spoke about third world debt, classism, and the superiority of mustard to mayonnaise.

"How was your meeting?" Sarah asked. "Women are always saying, 'How was your meeting?' Have you noticed?"

"It was canceled, yesterday afternoon. I should have gone home last night."

"Why didn't you?"

"HOW WAS YOUR MEETING?" she asked Michael, who ran on the treadmill next to hers as she walked. The hotel's health club was light and clear, windows and mirrors. Who likes windows better, and who likes mirrors, and what does that mean, if anything? Surely something other than the obvious... Although windows could serve vanity as well, providing an audience. The woman in the lavender workout suit experimented with different exercise machines as if trying on clothes, eyeing them, touching them, walking around them before climbing aboard.

"... so I walked out," Michael concluded.

Sarah worked her tongue over her teeth and pushed a strand of hair off of her forehead, trying for casual. "Tell me again why you walked out?"

He turned to her. "How could I stay after that?"

"Well, you're right, of course."

Michael turned face forward again. "I called Bill and told him to jerk their account."

"You had no choice."

"Damn straight!" Michael picked up speed, running, running from death as fast as he could.

Jennifer Lopez got married on the cover of *People*.

"Tell me more about Camila," Sarah said.

It wasn't good for her to know much about his meetings, she'd become anxious about something he did or didn't do. *You have to listen without listening,* her mother had said. Was that what Michael did.

SARAH KICKED OFF her shoes and sat on the hotel bed, the telephone receiver at her ear. "One pastrami sandwich, one hamburger well-done, extremely well-done, burnt, a Diet Coke, and two glasses of skim milk."

The heavy rain of Michael's shower erupted, and Sarah

opened the bathroom door to liberate steam. It sounded as if someone had dropped a bowling ball upstairs, and she waited as it rolled across the floor. The black leather shaving kit she'd given Michael sat on the heap in his suitcase, and his cellophane-covered-to-prevent-wrinkles suits hung in the closet above the tassel shoes she'd advised against buying.

She picked up a glossy magazine from a glass-topped table and paged through restaurants and tourist sites, before turning on CNN, where hundreds of Haitian refugees jumped from a bobbing wooden boat into heaving seas off the coast of Florida; they struggled toward shore, carrying nothing. The strongest among them — teenage boys — made it to land and clambered up steep, rocky cliffs to a highway, where they were arrested, the blades of the television helicopter spreading white-ringed whirlpools across green ocean, stirring fronds of palm. Brilliant Florida sunshine spilling over the scene like a taunt.

Sarah reached for the ringing phone. "You dialed 911?" an operator said.

"No."

"Is everything alright?"

"The Haitians . . ." Sarah said.

"As long as everything's alright."

A towel tucked at his waist, Michael entered the room as Sarah replaced the receiver, and picked up his watch from the bedside table, where the *New Yorker* lay. She'd introduced him to the *New Yorker,* the *New York Times,* NPR.

She studied the message light, which wasn't blinking, then rose, and walked to the window, peering through blinds at pigeons searching for crumbs at the foot of a trash can, the sky as gray as the birds. Last week she'd made inquiries about working at Amnesty International and the ACLU, but hesitated, because there was always one teeny little policy position with which she disagreed.

"How close is Haiti to Latin America, and what happened the day you went to the barbecue at Magdalena's father's ranch?"

Picking up a brush, Michael began jerking it through his hair. "Did you turn off the air conditioner?"

"Lowered it."

"I'm burning up." He sat on the bed. "We went horseback riding, late in the afternoon, Eric and Magdalena and me. And I. Would it be 'I'?" He removed the towel, putting on the white terry cloth robe.

Even with wet hair he looked great. Sitting on the bed beside him, she slid a finger behind his ear. "Who's Eric?"

"My best friend."

"How could you have a best friend I've never met?"

"You'll see." Wadding up the towel and lobbing it into the bathroom.

Someone pounded on the door, and Michael opened it to the acne-faced bellboy.

"You called 911?" the boy asked. He wore a little beige vest over his white shirt, the sleeves rolled up, and his brown, bowl-cut hair fell into his eyes, like her nephew's did. One look at her nephew as a baby and she knew she could kill for him, which must be how Michael felt about his children. Survival of the species.

"No."

"Is everything alright?"

"Is our dinner on the way?"

"I'll check on it, sir."

Michael closed the door and sank into the red and white striped chair.

"You could be holding me hostage," Sarah said. "They should have searched the room and interviewed me separately. Would you hold me hostage?"

"How much ransom would you bring?"

"In dollars or pesos?"

"Did you turn the air conditioner down again?"

"Finish about Eric, do *not* introduce another character until you tell me about Magdalena, unless you want to skip right to Camila."

"Eric was in my Peace Corps group, from New Jersey, and we hit it off right away, the first day of training. He was intense, political, a real do-gooder."

"I thought all volunteers were do-gooders."

"Some were avoiding Vietnam."

When Sarah was twenty, she'd been engaged to a Marine lieutenant who'd made no effort to avoid Vietnam; he was from Mississippi. One night he climbed aboard a helicopter by the Troi River for the last time. It mystified her that she could be reduced to racking sobs by this fact so many years later, but she preferred not to think about it.

Michael, too, had served in Vietnam, after the Peace Corps, but preferred not to talk about it. One night Sarah and Michael had a guest for dinner who went on at excruciating length about the virtues of the death penalty, until Michael exploded. *I have killed people, sometimes in self-defense, sometimes in attack, it's not to be taken lightly, this killing business, I will* never *forgive myself.* And when the man left they cleared the table and washed the dishes and remarked on the eclairs.

SARAH TRIED TO calculate how long she could lie nestled in the crook of Michael's arm before the crick in her neck became unbearable. Slowly, she slipped away, returning to the comfort of her own pillow, and took Michael's hand. The darkened room was illuminated by a flash of light from the street, then thrust into darkness again, as honking horns faded in intensity and frequency, a desultory midnight jazz.

"What did you like best about Eric?" she asked, rubbing her big toe across his.

The radio clock on the bedside table blinked loudly.

"He was a true believer."

"Now you hate people like that."

"We had our hearts broken."

She rested the back of her hand against his cheek.

"LADIES AND GENTLEMEN, OUR SECU-
RITY SYSTEM HAS INFORMED US THAT
THERE IS AN UNIDENTIFIED PROBLEM
IN THE HOTEL. PLEASE PROCEED TO THE
NEAREST EXIT AND LEAVE THE BUILDING.
LADIES AND GENTLEMEN, OUR SECURITY
SYSTEM HAS INFORMED US THAT THERE
IS AN UNIDENTIFIED PROBLEM IN THE
HOTEL. PLEASE PROCEED TO THE NEAR-
EST EXIT AND LEAVE THE BUILDING. LA-
DIES AND GENTLEMEN . . ."

Michael brushed his teeth first.

"OKAY, OKAY," MICHAEL SAID to Sarah the next morning as she pressed to hear more of the story. He loaded the
baggage into the trunk of the taxi and entered the backseat from the other side, the shut door muting the din of
rush-hour traffic, leftover drops of rain still clinging to
the windshield.

Sarah pulled on her seat belt; wide strips of gray tape
were applied across the torn seat cover, balls of white
foam spilling out of the wound.

"We'd been horseback riding for a couple of hours,"

Michael said, "and it was getting late, so I suggested we go home, but Magdalena didn't want to and begged to ride a little longer. She was like that. So we did. La Guardia." He leaned forward to make certain the driver had heard, then turned to Sarah. "We got lost. It was getting dark, nothing looked the same.

"We decided to spend the night and return in the morning — there was no choice — and started searching for a place to camp."

Who slept where.

SARAH STUDIED THE departure times on the airport monitor, fear of flying trumping all else, as Michael looked up from his newspaper. "Did you read this article about oil in Latin America? And the Chinese?"

A group of Marine recruits was herded into a hallway, then ordered to attention.

Searching the departures again, Sarah glanced at the clock, then eased a pill out of her purse and slipped it into her mouth. "Ang get jink wallah."

The high, adult water fountain wasn't working, and Sarah bent to drink from the low one, but the pill drifted to the front of her mouth, nearly escaping, so she held her head and back erect and squatted like a duck, waddling forward and sipping air until she got close enough for water. Water dribbled down her chin, and it took

several gulps and head tosses to accomplish the task before she stood, wiping a hand across her chin, brushing
past a little girl waiting in line behind her.

If she'd known she was going to be flying back she
would have worn her airplane shoes and loose-fitting,
elasticized waistband slacks, with cards in her purse that
said things like:

There are two billion flights a day,

The chances of being in a plane crash are one in a trillion,

Even though it may sound as if the engines have stopped,
I know the engines are running at all times,

Turbulence is a comfort issue, not a safety issue.

She eyed the other passengers in a racial-profiling sort
of way.

SARAH STEPPED ABOARD the plane, keeping her head
twisted to the right to avoid looking at the pilot in case he
wasn't white-haired, and passed into the dove gray cabin
where she was engulfed by the inside-of-a-plane smell.
Michael placed his suitcase in the overhead bin after
Sarah removed a blanket and pillow. "It's just an hour,"
he said.

She waited for him to squeeze into the middle seat,
his long legs bunched up around his chin, before she sat
down at the aisle and fastened her belt.

"We found a place to camp," Michael said, "and Eric
began gathering wood for a fire."

The safety instructions commanded Sarah's attention; Michael opened the *Economist*. "We have that charity dinner to go to tonight," he said.

"Could I wear the same dress?"

A long dark hair hung from the pillow on her lap.

SUNLIGHT STREAMED THROUGH the window as the plane emerged from the clouds, and the ice in her plastic glass swirled.

A loud thump.

"Bringing up the wheels," Michael said, not looking up from his magazine.

A crumpled paper cocktail napkin hopped across the floor. Another loud noise.

"Wing flaps," Michael said, turning a page.

The young uniformed pilot or copilot walked quickly through the cabin, stopping periodically to peer through windows at the plane's wing. He was chewing gum, and *People* magazine stuck out of his back pocket.

A stewardess tapped another stewardess on the elbow. "He wants us to return to our seats."

A woman across the aisle read a thick book because some people don't have the imagination to picture a plane spiraling earthward through hoops of fire.

. . .

SHE WOULD MAKE him tell her the rest of the story tonight. Buildings slung along the river lit up the night sky; a rosy gold cloud hovered above the city, and Michael honked at a hesitant driver as Sarah crossed her legs. No time to unpack; just time enough for Random and to change.

Michael leaned over to wipe off the dashboard where the toe of her shoe had touched it. When he was a boy, he said when he grew up he'd have enough money to go into a toy store and buy any toy he wanted.

"Is this the hotel with the good chocolate?" Sarah asked. "Who's going to be there?"

"They bought two tables — some people from sales, I think."

"What's it for?"

"Camps for sick children, or inner city youth. Eagles, maybe."

"Don't mention that we went to the play last weekend — we told Jared and Barbara you were sick and couldn't go to their party. Don't mention that a publisher's interested in my book because I don't want anyone to know in case it doesn't happen. Don't tell anyone how you feel about the election. Kim's pregnancy is a secret."

"What's Bob's wife's name?"

"Tallulah. Or Hallelujah. Make sure I don't sit next to Niles."

She pulled the visor down and looked in the mirror. "How'd the conference call go?"

"I think Jesse gets it."

"That was a good letter you wrote."

"You look great."

"You, too."

They pulled up to the Four Seasons, and Sarah stretched the fabric of her skirt across her stomach and buttoned it. Michael picked up a piece of lint from the floor of the car.

She wondered what Jacob was doing. And when Camila would unveil her plans for them.

MARGE AND PETER embraced them, as Sarah and Michael entered the huge chandeliered ballroom.

"*Much* too long!" Sarah said.

Marge took in Sarah's dress.

"You're sitting next to me," Niles said to Sarah, pulling out her chair. "And Dave couldn't make it, so Michael can sit on your other side."

Sarah turned to Michael, who sat down and reached for the rolls, taking one blond one and one brown one before going for butter. His leg shook the table, and she put a hand on his thigh to stop the bouncing. "When did you start shaking your leg?"

"I've been doing it as long as I can remember."

A taffeta-enshrouded woman brushed past them. "Now you can tell me what happened the night you and Eric and Magdalena spent out in the countryside," Sarah said. Who slept where.

"You've got to be kidding." He buttered the bread on his gold-rimmed plate, as Sarah leaned across him and glanced at the place card on his left. "Or you can chat with Betsy Stewart about her abdominal surgery," she said.

"We gathered firewood and built a fire." He took a bite. "Magdalena had brought some cheese and bread, just the heel of a loaf, I think." He took another bite and a few crumbs bounced off his black tie onto the white linen tablecloth. "And grapes, the irritating ones with seeds. That was dinner. We grabbed some bananas from a tree, but they weren't ripe, and we'd brought one of those wineskins — a bota — I forget whether they were sheep or goat skin — with water in it. It's beautiful country, which you notice more when you're not lost. Palm trees, bright red bougainvillea, plantain in the pastures, mountains in the distance, and deep, deep green, miles of emerald green, with stars everywhere."

When a waiter placed salmon appetizers in front of them, Sarah thanked him profusely, smiling warmly, inclusively.

"Did you get in much sailing over the summer?" she asked Niles. The salmon was rubbery.

"Have you seen the Christmas shop that opened in Marblehead?" Gail Cuddahy asked.

Were those Tahitian pearls?

"We decided to go to sleep, figuring on an early start," Michael said, "and I tried, but the ground was hard, and rocky, and it was cold, we burrowed under our ponchos.

They call them ruanas — some are gorgeous — made of alpaca, really nice wool. I slept a little."

"Around one o'clock in the morning I heard something — Magdalena and Eric were trying to wrestle some guy to the ground — I thought he might be crazy or a thief, but it turned out he was foraging for food. Together, we were able to subdue him and tie him up, but not before he got a slug in to my right jaw."

When Sarah knocked her silver spoon to the floor, a waiter materialized and handed her another. She didn't know whether she was kicking a portion or a table leg and shifted position.

"We couldn't figure out what to do with him — if we let him go, he could have come back and murdered us in our sleep, or stolen what little food we had left, so we gave him some water and cheese, and decided to take turns sleeping and watching him. He was curious about us, wanted to know who we were, where we were from, everything."

One waiter removed their appetizer plates, another deposited herb-roasted chicken.

"How are your children?" Sarah asked Gail. The chicken was rubbery.

"How long were you in the hospital after the operation?" Michael asked Betsy, her floral perfume dense and far-reaching.

The garlic mashed potatoes weren't bad.

"He wasn't crazy after all," Michael said. "He was a guerrilla, on his way back to a camp in the mountains."

"A guerrilla? Spelled g-u-e-r-r-i-l-l-a?"

Michael nodded. "Eric was fascinated, wanted to know all about his life, his beliefs. I think the guy must have thought we were harmless, or maybe he was just so hungry and cold he didn't know or care what he told us, not that he told us anything that he shouldn't, nothing that revealing, and everyone knew the rebels had strongholds in the mountains. He was impressive, a college graduate, from a well-to-do family. Idealistic and charismatic. There was a horrible disparity between the rich and poor in those days, still is, and he was one of those people who feels personally, deeply wounded when he witnesses injustice. Like Eric."

"What was Magdalena doing during all of this?"

"Listening. The guy was explaining how the rebels were going to help the campesinos who were being ripped off by the landowners, and Eric got into a thing about Marx with him.

"Eric and this guy spent hours talking, but I drifted off to sleep."

"Magdalena?"

"I told you, I went to sleep."

An army of synchronized, bow-tie-wearing waiters marched into the ballroom bearing silver trays of sorbet — peach, lemon, and raspberry.

"When I woke up the next morning, Eric, Magdalena, and the guerrilla were all asleep."

". . . and so, ladies and gentlemen, it's with great pleasure that I introduce tonight's host, Cherry Griffith, an-chor of *News at Five*."

Michael put an arm around Sarah's chair, and she ap-plauded with the others.

"What happened next?" she asked. Cherry was frosted blonde.

"I woke everyone up, and we let the guy go," Michael whispered. "By that point it was clear he wasn't any kind of a threat; it's as if we were all buddies."

Cherry continued speaking: "blah blah blah inspiration blah blah blah children blah blah blah blah blah hope blah blah blah blah generosity blah blah blah blah . . ."

"What about Magdalena?"

"You're getting ahead."

"Shh," someone said.

THEY WAVED GOOD-BYE to the hand-holding Gartners as Michael held the car door open for Sarah. The Gart-ners probably had a loving marriage, overflowing with tenderness. Sarah got into the car, kicked off her shoes, and unfastened the button at her waist.

"Could you believe that guy at the table behind us?" Michael asked, turning the ignition.

"I felt sorry for his wife." Sarah had been humiliated numerous times by her first husband, an alcoholic. One friend thought she'd married him out of rebelliousness, another knew better. "He's the sexiest man I've ever met," the woman said. It was almost still the sixties, and marrying a stone mason was what you did, flowers in your hair. The alcoholism blossomed later, her fault.

"The Gartners are getting divorced," Michael said, "but he hasn't told her yet."

"Why?"

"I didn't ask."

Sarah had once marveled at the stability of corporate marriages, until someone pointed out that no one wanted to divide the money. Michael had told her he'd rather be broke and lonely than live with someone who . . . What was it she'd done? It was, and remained, murky. Perhaps she didn't know everything. Whatever it was, two years ago Michael had announced his intention to leave Sarah, until he spent an afternoon in their beloved backyard a few days later: *I realized we'd lose EVERYTHING.*

Michael was capable of saying it's over. Michael had found himself capable of firing people on many occasions, and Sarah knew before he did when he was going to do it; a subconscious decision would be made, then she would begin to hear a long litany of complaints, going back years, about the employee, who, it turned out, had *never* done anything right. *I don't believe in sacrificing the flock for the sake of the lamb.* He built the case, argued with himself, tried to push through the guilt attending the most difficult part of his job. The employee's part, of course, was harder, and their spouses would write about that.

Rain splattered the windshield, and the wipers cut a swath of clean glass through the drops slowly and erratically as they pulled away from the hotel. Had Michael had further contact with Camila without telling her?

I'm the dog who positions herself between her master and the door so abandonment won't occur without warning.

"MICHAEL DOESN'T WANT to tell me any more about Magdalena and seems to know next to nothing about Camila," Sarah said, standing beside the large WE DO NOT SELL OXYCONTIN sign in front of the pharmacy counter. "It's possible they're in touch. He keeps changing the subject, leaving the room, having to work. Why is it so charged?"

"You have to admit it's awkward," Rachel said, "telling your wife about your first love." She scooped up an Imodium A-D packet from a nearby shelf and put down her briefcase, reading the back of the package.

"I was thinking maybe it wasn't love," Sarah said. "More like your run-of-the-mill lust."

"I'd keep my eye on Camila," Rachel said.

Shifting her books to the other arm, Sarah counted the people ahead of them — eight. "What are we getting today?"

"Ativan, Cipro, Prevacid, steroids, and Neurontin.

"I need to finish my shrinking company benefits article by Friday," Rachel said, glancing at a plastic pillbox: M T W TH F S SUN. "Remember the woman I met in the

Dana-Farber waiting room, whose husband had bone cancer? He's howling in pain at some nursing home and they keep forgetting to bring his morphine and don't respond to his calls, so he screams to be taken home but his wife can't move him because it takes three people to turn him over and she doesn't have help. She wants to slip him some morphine, but she'd be arrested."

"They could move to Oregon," the woman behind them said.

Sarah had been to Oregon, but to the eastern part, east of the Cascade Range, where it's sunny, not doom and gloom like the rest. Beautiful, nice skiing, although recently they'd discovered an Al-Qaeda cell there. Sarah and Michael had visited a friend at a resort, a golf community, where everything was clean and tidy and gave a sense that things were under control.

The bent, white-haired customer at the prescription counter turned and walked away when told the price of heart medication.

Rachel glanced at the clock. "Now I take Ativan during the day, too."

LETTER TO SARAH —

Brazil
. . . I hate when we fight, I can't wait to get home . . .
Michael

SARAH SAT ON the black and gold striped chair on the oriental rugs outside Michael's office near the busy bank of secretaries clustered in the center of the large room. A bird at the window flapped its wings, trying to get in.

When Sarah had a secretary, she apologized for giving him work.

She wouldn't leave until Michael concluded the story.

Voices emerged from his office, the door to which was ajar.

"Forget it." (Michael)

"They might walk." (unidentified male)

"Let 'em." (Michael)

"Did you want me to cancel your trip to Colombia?" (Michael's secretary)

"Why?"

"Sarah feels it's unnecessary."

"MAGDALENA DISAPPEARED." Michael bit into his turkey sandwich on wheat with tomato but no lettuce.

Sarah placed her paper plate with tuna fish and chips back on his mahogany desk.

When his phone rang, he shook his head and held up his hand to indicate he wasn't going to answer.

"About two months after the night we got lost," he said. He leaned back in his chair, almost hitting the shelf of photographs behind him — photographs of Michael sailing, mountain climbing, horseback riding in the jungles of Latin America, on his Harley, and a photograph of Sarah, Lisa, and Random.

"What happened during the two months before Magdalena disappeared?"

He ate a stalk of celery, the sound of it filling the room.

"We spent a lot of time together," he said, pushing his plate away. "One day she was gone." He rubbed his temples. "We were supposed to meet at a restaurant for dinner."

The ringing phone.

"I thought you lived in a slum."

"I did, but we met downtown, in nice places, she would take the bus into town to meet me — her father didn't like her being involved with a Norte Americano." He folded his napkin. "She took a lot of risks to be with me. I've only recently come to realize that."

Guilt, that's why he hadn't been able to talk about it. She'd never known a man so vulnerable to guilt; God knows what it would lead him to do. His alcoholic grandfather, head of the household when his father was overseas. No one but Michael to protect his mother.

Or Vietnam. Michael had been involuntarily hospitalized for depression when he returned from Vietnam, grabbed right off the plane, some unmentionable episode in the Delta having pushed him over the brink. After the hospital there were dreams, he'd said, and wild swingings of his machete in the middle of the night, until he removed it from the house. To say he didn't like looking back was a trivializing understatement.

"What did it look like?" she asked.

"The restaurant?"

"I need to picture it."

Voices could be heard outside the window.

"It was rustic-looking, with nice views of the city — it's a modern city, in spite of the old-world Spanish feel — and through the windows you could see some residential apartment buildings and a few stand-alone homes. It rained at first that night — I remember because I waited for her so long, and kept looking out the window, and the streets were shiny, slick."

His secretary entered and put some papers on his desk.

It would have been better if Michael and Magdalena's relationship had died of its own accord, a gradual accretion of resentment and disinterest, nothing unresolved.

The secretary left.

"There were exposed wooden beams, traditional pottery, and people ate steaks and fried plantain and yuccas, and beer."

"Yuccas?"

"A tuber plant, stringy. Pure starch. A potato, a member of the potato family, awful." He tapped his foot. "And the sound of banging on tables; they wore heavy rings, and banged them on the table when they wanted the waiter, but I don't think they do that anymore.

"She never showed, and I was frantic, and drove my jeep out towards her father's ranch, thinking there'd been an accident, but I didn't find anything. I didn't actually go to the ranch — I was no longer welcome there — but the next night, when I still hadn't heard from her, I drove back." He looked up at Sarah, and her need for visual details. "It was a normal-looking hacienda — stucco walls, orange-tiled roof, with beautiful plants hanging on the verandas. Ranch gear lying around — lariats, saddles — there was a courtyard.

"Her father hadn't seen her since the previous afternoon and was furious; he thought I'd had something to do with her disappearance." He glanced at Sarah. "He wore a wide-brimmed straw hat from the llanos, kind of a cross between a Panamanian and a cowboy hat, and a working jacket, slacks, and work boots, like Wellingtons." Michael picked up a pen and drummed the desk. "The campesinos, the guys who worked the ranch, were barefoot."

He stood and paced. "We searched everywhere." He stopped and held up his hands. "The ranch was surrounded by pastures separated by fences and tree lines, with mountains in the distance.

"Lots of people helping. We looked for a long time . . ." He sat, as his secretary came in.

"Barossa on line four," she said.

"I'll call him back."

The secretary left, and Michael tapped his foot. "Her father resigned himself to her death."

Sarah put her hand on his thigh to stop his shaking leg.

"I wrote to her father a couple of years after I got back to the States, to see if there was any news, but he never replied."

But now that Camila has entered the picture you could find out. Or perhaps he already had. This was a question she could have asked if she weren't afraid of the answer.

Angry voices outside the window grew louder.

"What happened to Eric?" Sarah asked

"He'd already left, everybody in our group, but I'd extended."

"To be with Magdalena?"

He folded the debris from his lunch and threw it in the trash.

"Why didn't you and Eric stay in touch?"

His secretary walked in. "Roy's here."

Michael looked at his watch. "Ten minutes."

"Things went weird after Magdalena and I got together," he said. "Before that, Eric and I had been inseparable."

She'd find Eric, she could learn things. She should brace herself. She studied the photograph of the young man on a horse. "In New York, you said you and Eric had your hearts broken."

Tapping his pen on the desk, he looked out the window. "We wanted to save the world." He turned back to his desk, tapped some more. "We accomplished nothing measurable." He spun his empty milk carton, then picked it up and read it. Setting the container down next to a sheaf of papers, he glanced at the column of figures on the page. "Our numbers this quarter are great."

Outside, people were screaming.

"DO YOU THINK all terror is fear of death?" Sarah asked.

Still wearing the name tag from his research conference, Jacob put down the plastic menu covered with colorful pictures of ice cream sundaes and chocolate fudge cake. His panel had gone well, he said, and Sarah had seen the gaggle of females hovering around him afterward.

The restaurant featured orange walls which had, fortunately, aged and dulled. In a corner booth, a soldier held hands with a young woman.

"Are hospitals scary because we anticipate pain and anxiety, or because of death?" Sarah continued. "If death is the thing we're afraid of, what is it about death that frightens us?"

The waitress, wearing a pink uniform with a white paper apron and cap, poured Jacob's coffee. "It's the dying, not the death," she said before moving to the next table.

"Then it's the pain and anxiety," Sarah said. "But take out the dying part. Let's say you're guaranteed a painless, comfortable, quick death. Now, is death still scary? And, if so, why? Michael doesn't want to die because he doesn't want it to end, he mostly thinks it's fun, but I think I'm afraid because you do it alone — the ultimate separation anxiety. And it could entail an eternity of loneliness."

"Settlements on the Gaza Strip," someone in the booth behind them said.

"Instead of writing, I worry about Magdalena and Camila," Sarah said. She drew a stick figure in orange crayon on the paper place mat, added curls.

"Magdalena's in the past. Nobody seems to know where she is anyway. Camila's where you should focus."

"Michael will be drawn back. In fact, he may already be in touch with Magdalena, and I'm well versed in the high school reunion phenomenon. It makes them feel young, and Michael's desperate to feel young." Tossing the crayon, Sarah looked over her shoulder. "I'm here to bring the book you need." She reached down and handed him the battered and torn *How to Love Your Teenager.*

Jacob leafed through the book. "Talking with you gives me a headache." He looked up at her. "In a good way."

"I think people with children must feel differently about death," she said.

He put the book down. "Who were you before Michael?"

"A woman who worked in offices for twenty years. When I saw an ad recently for that TV series about housewives, I was interested, and identified with the women, or the idea of the women, and wondered how this happened, that I'm identifying with housewives."

She looked over her shoulder.

"It happens subtly," Sarah said. "I was working when Michael and I got married; he was looking for something new then, and got a good job, and was rapidly promoted.

"One night we had his direct reports over for dinner, and there was this one wife in particular who was anxious and kept asking Michael how the company was doing and was so intent on making sure her husband's job was not in jeopardy, and that's when I understood what it was to be economically dependent on another human being. I have become that woman." A big breath.

"Michael got the offer to come here, and we thought it would be a good opportunity for me to write, but he's making money and I'm not, so it makes sense that I handle the dishes, the bills, the plumber, the electrician, the dog-walking, the social calendar, and get frightened if he's mad at me." She took a sip of Jacob's coffee. "There have been serious erosions into my freedom of speech, much of it self-inflicted."

A loud siren blared, and people looked up in alarm and began leaving their tables.

"What kind of job did you have?" Jacob asked.

"It was in Washington, funding artists, reigning over fierce battles between the avant-garde and traditionalists; I don't think anyone says 'avant-garde' anymore, do they.

"Josip Novakovich wrote a novel in which a teacher says to his students, something like, 'And that, children, is art. Art is what makes life good.'" Should she explain to Jacob that "art" meant literature, music, film, etcetera, as well as the visual arts. "I was doing something that mattered."

She couldn't believe she'd said that. People filed out of the restaurant as the siren sounded.

"I earned more than Leo, my first husband," she said, "a stone mason who could make you weep with a description of the feel of stone in your hand. He would be out of work for big chunks of time, and we did okay, but there was that feeling in the pit of my stomach wondering if the bills would wait until payday."

Their waitress took off her apron and folded it across the back of a chair before joining the exiting crowd.

"He left me for a woman he met in the unemployment line," Sarah said, "and left her for a woman he met at rehab."

She turned Jacob's coffee cup around. "I suppose you'd like to talk."

The lights dimmed.

Jacob told Sarah about the trouble he'd gotten into as a teenager (drugs and minor criminal activity), the art school that saved him, the older couple — intellectual and worldly — who'd taken an interest. Youthful rebelliousness channeled into benign bohemianism.

The woman sitting with the soldier began laughing, tears streaming down her face.

· · ·

"HI, SWEETIE!" Michael said to Rachel, bending over to kiss her on the cheek. Rachel sat on Sarah and Michael's graying white sofa next to Sarah; Michael had come home from work — wearing the black suit Sarah liked — to drive Rachel to her blood test so Sarah could wait for the cable guy.

Michael kissed Sarah on the forehead, brushing past the violets Rachel had brought them from her garden.

"Sit down," Rachel said. "We have a few minutes." Her button said HUNGRY FOR NATIONAL LEADERSHIP.

Sarah put the grocery list Rachel had given her on the coffee table; Rachel had indicated the order in which grocery items were to be removed from the shelves, aisle by aisle.

Michael sat.

"I need to ask you a few questions," Rachel said, wearing the pretty pink linen blouse that could be wrinkled and it was okay. "Were you in love with Magdalena?"

Michael's eyes darted between Rachel and Sarah.

"I had nothing to do with this . . ." Sarah said, throwing her hands in the air.

"She had nothing to do with this," Rachel said. "I'm tired of the pussyfooting around."

Michael looked out the window — it was raining, the quiet, steady sheets kind — then back at Rachel. "You have to understand how disorienting it was to be a North American thrust into such an alien environment. You lose your bearings."

"What did she look like?"

"She had blue eyes. Startling with the black hair." He glanced at Sarah. "I remember Eric commenting on them."

"Did you and Magdalena live together?" Rachel asked.

"Sometimes she would tell her father she was visiting a girlfriend and stay for a while."

"Let's abandon the Q and A format," Rachel said. "Give me a paragraph on Magdalena."

Michael looked at Sarah, then back at Rachel, who had a way of cocking her head, thrusting her chin forward, fixing her gaze . . . No one else could get away with this.

"Her mother died when she was a kid, and she was mostly raised by an old Indian woman who cooked for them, and other ranch hands." He looked at Sarah, then back at Rachel again. "She had a favorite horse, a Paso Fino; she was good with horses. Not domestic, read a lot." He looked around the room. "What else? She was a chain-smoker, restless as a colt. Loved practical jokes, could always get people to follow, contagious." He was talking faster. "It must be time to go." He looked at his watch.

Rachel shook her head.

Michael sat back again, thought. "As a child, she had a bird, a pet, that she kept in a bamboo cage, a little bird, delicate, maybe a sparrow or something. She called it Mija."

"Mija?" Rachel asked.

"Dear one, sweetie, love. Technically, 'my daughter.'

She was only eight and the bird was her first responsibility, and she loved it more than she'd ever loved anything; she described how she tried to comb it with one of those tiny plastic combs girls have for their dolls."

Sarah averted her eyes, which landed on the wooden sculpture Rachel had brought them from a trip to Africa. Did the protrusion of the woman's belly indicate she was pregnant.

"One day Magdalena and her sister went to visit their aunt but there was a huge storm, so they had to spend the night, and then another night, and no one fed the bird, so when they came home, it had died."

"It wasn't her fault," Rachel said.

"She cried when she told it."

Sarah felt as if she'd had too much caffeine, although she hadn't had any. She had a theory about sexual attraction. Take Elvis Presley, he was handsome, masculine, sexy, vital, oozing testosterone, but vulnerable, a kid trying to please, trying not to get hurt. Every woman in the world wanted to sleep with him and mother him at the same time. And Marilyn Monroe — men wanted to sleep with her and take care of her, some kind of parental instinct mixed up with sexual attraction.

"We can't go until you answer the most important thing," Rachel said. "Tell me about Camila." When Sarah and Rachel went out to eat, Rachel questioned the waiter at length, insisted on sampling the wine, sent back imperfect food.

Michael came to his feet. "The only thing to know about Camila is that she's been without a father too long. We're going."

He didn't know anything about Camila.

Rachel exchanged a glance with Sarah and gathered her things. She was scheduled for a CAT scan later. *I hate CAT scans,* she'd said. *All the radiation can cause problems years down the line.*

"I've had some thoughts about your business," Rachel said, as she followed Michael out the door.

Once a deer had jumped the fence into their yard and tried to hide among the trees in the back. "Don't force him," the animal control guy said. "Wait until dusk, he'll move on his own."

THE DETAILS WERE SKETCHY, Jacob moving in and out of focus, pressing close.

Sarah opened her eyes with a start and stared at the midnight ceiling. She turned and looked at Michael, sleeping lumpy-shadowed beside her.

She kicked off the covers.

"DON'T LEAN SO far forward!" Michael shouted back at Sarah as their helmets crashed, his voice above the rushing wind muffled through metal. The sapphire blue Harley climbed the hill behind the house, and Sarah hugged

Michael, aiming her chin at the top of his left shoulder; helmets banged.

They bumped over a pothole, but she landed comfortably on the wide black leather seat, and was reminded of posting at a trot as a child, when she'd been afraid of horses but chose the one named Satan anyway. She drew horses, dreamt of horses, named imaginary horses, and selected horse pictures instead of a transistor radio, like her brother had when they traveled to Japan and were allowed one gift. Later, she wrote stories about horses who were beautiful and spirited with flying manes carrying their riders to freedom. If she had a daughter, she wouldn't laugh at her crush on horses.

Cresting the hill at Farrington Street — leafy sunshine intercut with Victorian houses — they began the descent, approaching the right onto Blayton at the cheese shop, and in spite of instructions to the contrary, she instinctively leaned away from the curb and the rising road as the bike bent into the turn. Michael gunned the motor, and they were straight out; she heard a vehicle on their tail but didn't look as they passed a parked car with a bumper sticker written in Arabic.

"I love you!" Sarah shouted. The wind hurled the words back in her face as she held calves well clear of hot steel pipes, and leaned forward.

. . .

SARAH WOULD NOT only find Eric, she'd meet with Camila.

The man wasn't paying attention to Sarah and took a sort of stick and lay it across Sarah and Michael's bed. She stood between him and the bedroom door, for quick escape, although he was older, overweight, and she could probably outrun him.

"How long have you had the mattress?" he asked, as he took what appeared to be measurements of the valleys in the mattress. He walked to the next side and measured again, as Random followed, sniffing his left boot.

"Seven months."

"Something's definitely wrong." He walked to another side and lay the stick across. He was bald, with glasses, a cellophane-coated cigar peering out of his shirt pocket.

Jets roared overhead. Were they military planes?

"Have you been flipping it?" he asked.

"Once."

"People underestimate the importance of flipping."

"How often should you do it?"

"Every month for the first six months, after that is less important."

"Turning it in circles? Like clockwise?"

"And then over, like a pancake." He consulted his notes. "They say you want reimbursement to go towards a Stearns and Foster."

"Is that a good mattress?"

"It depends on what you want."

Random put his front paws on the windowsill and barked at a passerby as white jet contrails cut across blue sky.

"Shouldn't we have firm mattresses, for our backs?" Sarah asked.

"It depends. My wife has a back problem and bought a really stiff mattress, but it's so uncomfortable I can't sleep."

"Shouldn't we sleep on our backs?" she asked. "I thought that was best, but someone told me we should sleep on our sides, in the fetal position, to stretch the back."

"I don't know how much longer I can stand it," he said.

Jacob's wife had a back problem. How would that affect things? "Are Shif mattresses good?"

"Shifman. They can be. Some tend to give a little more. I believe this mattress was damaged when they carried it upstairs."

"They folded it."

Did mattresses affect dreams? Sarah had a recurring nightmare that she slept in a bed with a small baby — sometimes the baby was no larger than her thumb — and that she rolled over and crushed the baby, or spent the night trying not to roll over and crush the baby.

"I saw a mattress once, just a few blocks from here, you wouldn't believe," he said. "It was as if an elephant slept on one side. The woman in the house said she was single, just an itty-bitty thing, couldn't have weighed more than ninety pounds." He walked to the next side of the mattress and bent over with his stick. "Another couple, over in Jamaica Plain, turned the mattress like they were supposed to, but then changed the direction they slept, so they were sleeping in the same dents they had just made. King-size beds are square, you know."

Random jumped on the bed to watch.

"Is this your full-time job?" Sarah asked as more planes passed. Why are there so many?

"For ten years. What do you do?"

"I'm a writer. People don't understand why I don't get more done; they don't understand about things like this."

"What are you writing about?"

"The intersection of humor and terror."

He didn't look up from his notes.

"Or, if you prefer, about a man and a woman and another woman."

He nodded and put his papers in his pocket. "You have to consider springs, their density, etcetera, and mattress pads, which can make a difference. And pillow-top mattress pads, they can sag, too, you know. Mattress pads should be washed frequently, people are allergic.

"You shouldn't go to bed with your hair wet — mold on the pillow case." He removed his glasses to rub his eye. "I'll tell you what I'm going to do, I'm going to approve your reimbursement." He replaced his glasses. "You must promise to flip."

you ask
why I didn't sleep
last night and I
say it's the anniversary
of my fiancé's death and you
don't say anything or look
up but continue
eating your cereal and I think
yes

"WASHINGTON, D.C." Bringing the phone from the nightstand to the bed, Sarah sat cross-legged in a large mattress sag and leafed through *The Things They Carried* while she waited, pausing to admire a particularly elegant sentence. The first time she'd read the book she'd been in Vermont, accompanying Michael on a fly-fishing trip. Sarah remembered where she was when she read seminal books, the way people remember where they were when they learned Kennedy had been assassinated. The way she remembered looking out her dorm window the morning her fiancé drove away when he left for Vietnam.

"The Peace Corps," she said into the phone, turning pages.

"Please hold for the number."

Sarah hung up and redialed "I'd like some information."

If Magdalena carried the emotional weight in Michael's life that Jonathan did in hers, Sarah was doomed.

PREGNANT WOMEN DRAGGING toddlers roamed the shop; Sarah had scrambled to look up baby stores in the yellow pages when Rachel told her their task. Colorful toys and strollers were displayed amidst infant clothing.

"*I've* been engaged," a woman said into her cell phone.

When she was in college, all Sarah had wanted to do when she graduated was have a baby, and she had assisted her pregnant sister-in-law, folding the soft white diapers (they were cloth then) into neat stacks on the changing table. Later, when she visited her brother and sister-in-law again, the baby had been born and was crawling around the house getting into various sorts of trouble, preceded and followed by tears and anger. This was a different thing from the neat stacks.

"They have no record of Eric," Sarah said, holding up a pink baby bonnet for Rachel's approval. You'd think baby bonnets wouldn't be big enough for an adult. Yellow butterflies and rose kittens hung from mobiles above cribs.

"Not pink," Rachel said, stroking other selections. "Why are you looking for Eric?"

"He was Michael's best friend, and if Michael won't tell me more about Magdalena and Camila, maybe Eric will."

"The Peace Corps's a bureaucracy, too." Rachel examined a blue cap. "You're barking up the wrong tree. It's Camila." She studied the bonnet. "Not only do bald heads get cold at night when you're trying to sleep, it turns out that when we smile or frown our scalps move."

"Why'd you have your head shaved?" Sarah asked.

"Losing your hair all at once is better than little by little. The illusion of control." She picked up a small yellow cap and held it to her cheek, turning to Sarah. "There's something fishy about Eric."

A little girl and boy leaned against their mother, so delicious you wanted to . . .

Sarah brushed a strand of wig hair out of Rachel's eyes as a saleswoman crawled along the floor on her hands and knees in search of something.

E-MAIL FROM MICHAEL —

Sarah, where are you? I've called four times . . .

"WHAT'S GOING ON?" Lisa dropped her backpack on the floor. "Dad sounded odd when he asked me to dinner." Two earrings hung from her left lobe, one from the right.

Sarah hugged her stepdaughter and closed the door behind her.

Tossing her denim jacket over the back of the wing chair, Lisa, with not nearly enough body fat for comfort, plopped down on the hard rosewood Chinese chair and stroked the arm. "Is this new?"

A large mongrel insect, a cross between a fly and a mosquito, sat on the floor next to the oriental rug, and Sarah squashed it with the toe of her shoe, only belatedly remembering Lisa's on-again, off-again Buddhist leanings. If they were in her home, insects were fair game; she left them alone outside, and didn't believe in preemptive strikes. She scooped up the flattened, blood-splattered insect with a Kleenex and carried it to the trash can beneath what looked like a bullet hole in the mudroom wall.

Random ran in circles around Lisa, who flirted aggressively with him.

"Your father will be down in a minute," Sarah said, folding her legs under her on the soiled white sofa. Random jumped to join her, adding fresh mud to the old.

Lisa and Michael had been stones rubbed together during Lisa's adolescence. She'd come to live with them when she was fifteen, staying until she left for the University of California at Santa Cruz, and now she worked at Tomorrow.com, while studying to be a social worker at night.

"Rick's an idiot," Lisa said, standing and pacing in her high-top, black-laced boots. Her short skirt appeared to be pieced together from an eclectic assortment of rags; a BlackBerry peered out of her pocket. "We're supposed to be organizing for the protest, and he decides we should have an office retreat, sitting around navel-gazing and talking about process on the Cape."

"Which protest?"

"In Washington."

"Against what?"

"Globalization, capitalism, exploitation of the environment, prisoners' rights, the demolition of the Florida Street Café."

Michael had once accompanied Sarah to a mammoth demonstration in Washington. The overwhelming, transforming sensation of being a speck in a swirling sea of humanity.

"When did you shave off your hair?" Sarah asked Lisa.

"It was a distracting symbol of female pulchritude." She turned to Sarah. "Did Dad tell you what Mom did with our cat when she died?"

Michael ran down the stairs and into the living room buckling his belt, his newly showered hair flat and streaming. "Hi, sweetie."

Random jumped down from the sofa and stuck his rump up in the play position.

"Where'd you get that shirt?" Lisa asked.

"I'll have Shanghai pan-fried noodles with beef," he said.

Sarah and Michael had gone to a Chinese restaurant on their second date, and she'd fallen for him in a big way and was too nervous to say a word, so he'd had to do all the talking. The next day he called to say he'd never had such a wonderful time.

"Vegetarian dumplings," Lisa said.

Sarah walked to the phone, past dead white tulips drooping over the lip of the vase like fallen soldiers.

"I ASKED FOR EXTRA pancakes and plum sauce," Sarah said, batting her arm around the inside of the carryout bag, in their kitchen, where a fax machine purred next to the Centrum Silver vitamins. Lisa opened cartons.

"I have a daughter," Michael said. "Another one."

Sarah ceased flailing about in the sack.

"Didn't you ask for chopsticks?" Lisa asked, looking at Sarah. "I thought you liked chopsticks."

Michael looked at Lisa. "I said I have — "

"Let's sit down," Sarah said.

A noise outside like thunder, but not thunder, coming closer.

They brought their plates to the dining room, and Sarah sat at the part of the table where you have to put one leg on one side of the table leg and one leg on the other. Her paper plate perched at an angle on the uneven surface where the middle leaf of the table connected to its neighbor, and she arranged her heaviest food downhill.

The house shuddered as the convoy of olive green trucks passed.

Lisa had spilled rice on the place mats, the same mauve color as the abstract painting, which was only a nude man if you looked closely.

"A man on the subway said the president knows more than we do," Lisa said, "and that we should trust him." She poured hoisin sauce from the tiny cup onto her dumplings. "Corporations have destroyed this country."

Random sat under the table awaiting errors.

"You can't be *for* jobs and *against* business," Michael said, mixing his noodles in sauce. "Paul Tsongas said that."

Lisa glanced at her watch. "There's an important boxing match tonight. Oscar De La Hoya." She cut into her vegetarian dumpling. "Remember the time we drove from LA to San Francisco and I read my diary out loud? I skipped parts."

"I know," Sarah said. "I was sitting in the backseat, remember? Leaning over the front seat." She'd never told Michael what she'd read in the skipped parts. The dark side.

"Was there something you wanted to say?" Sarah asked Michael, as he guided a forkful of food toward his mouth.

He held the fork in midair. "About the meeting? I thought I told you." He ate.

"Rick's a jerk," Lisa said.

"You have a sister," Michael said. "I didn't know she existed until a couple of weeks ago — she's the daughter of a woman I was involved with while I was in the Peace Corps."

Lisa was expressionless.

"She can't take your place, of course," Sarah said. "You will always be special. Not that she's not nice, I'm sure. I'm sure she's very nice. But not *you*. You are unique and —"

"When do I meet her?" Lisa asked.

"SHE'S COMING TO Boston in two weeks," Michael said to his mother, who studied her uneaten Big Mac.

"Your granddaughter," he tried, turning to his father, who continued eating his chocolate sundae with nuts, looking as if he were going to slide out of the booth. "For a journalism conference," Michael said. "She's a journalist — aren't you going to eat your hamburger first?"

Sarah ate one of Michael's french fries. She looked forward to Camila's arrival. *Now we'll find out who she is.*

Outside, a man in a blue Chevrolet overshot the drive-thru and gave his order to a trash can. The playground looked like fun, particularly the giant red slide; why wasn't anyone using it.

"What did you say her name was?" Michael's mother asked.

"Camila."

"How'd you find out about her?"

"She called, she'd done quite a bit of research. She's very determined, like her . . ." Michael put his hands around his filet of fish sandwich, then put it down, reaching for his Coke.

Outside, three men placed small rugs on the grass, knelt in the same direction, and prayed.

"I knew a Camila once," Michael's father said. "She was from Baltimore."

"That was Camille," Michael's mother said. "She was a tramp."

A man at the end of the left line to place orders moved to the end of the line at the right, which looked as if it were moving more quickly.

"I knew another woman they named a hurricane after," Michael's father said.

The man at the end of the right line moved to the end of the left line, which looked as if it were moving more quickly.

"HOW CAN THEY get away with calling this a yacht club," Michael whispered to Sarah, "when there aren't any yachts?"

Sarah's parents — now it was dinner — sat across the table behind peach-tinted petals.

"There isn't water," Michael whispered.

"What should we call her?" Sarah's mother asked.

"I remember that hurricane," Sarah's father said.

"That was Camille," her mother said. "Like your second cousin." She rolled her eyes at Sarah and mouthed "floozie." "Does she still live in Baltimore?"

A drop of wax slid down the side of the white candle, and condensation from the water glass sank into the linen tablecloth. A clock gonged.

OKAY, JACOB SAID, in response to Sarah's pestering in front of the kangaroo cage at the zoo.

As you well know, I was born and raised in Brooklyn. Clue Brooklyn. I went to City College, where I met my wife — she was in theater then.

Yes, beautiful. Still is.

It's not that I don't want to talk about her, it seems wrong.

We worked in Manhattan for ten years, until I got the job here. Most of our friends are there. It takes longer to make friends when you're married.

My brother's a teacher in San Francisco, and a bocci champion. A son and daughter.

The most tears shed was the day Lennie was born.

My father died of a heart attack three years ago. My mother plays canasta and volunteers at the hospital.

My favorite childhood toy was a beautiful painted wooden Easter egg that my grandmother had sent.

No, you don't play with it exactly, but admire it. I suppose Michael had miniature soldiers.

Nothing wrong with cowboys and Indians.

Of course, you had a small wooden dog on wheels that followed you everywhere.

Because my wife's allergic.

"There are days when that's the only proof that God exists," Sarah said. "Dogs."

When does Camila arrive?

"Tomorrow night."

The television emitted green images of bombs dropping on buildings.

PART TWO

"I'd planned to die in this house," Michael said, bending over to stick a shoehorn into the heel of his black shoe. It pained him that his grandmother hadn't lived long enough to see the house, a symbol of his success.

Sarah leaned toward the mirror to apply brown lipstick over red. "The apartments on high floors have river views, and it would be more secure. I would feel safe when you travel."

Michael tied his shoelaces, then stood and put on his jacket.

"I could chat with the concierge when you're out of town during terrorist attacks," Sarah said. "Did I mention I'd feel safe?"

"We'd have to sell the house." He brushed off his lapel. "Does this tie work?"

"Think cool colors with cool colors, warm with warm. You're wearing a blue suit. Is that cool or warm?"

The brown tie slumped to the chair when he dropped it.

She took a sideways glance in the mirror, patting her sucked-in stomach. "Are you sure you don't want me to go to the airport with you?"

SITTING ALONE IN the backseat of a taxi on the way to the restaurant, Sarah said nothing.

When she was a child, her mother had explained that being one of three friends was difficult, someone always feeling left out. Her mother didn't know how to hold hands, but was wise.

"HOW WAS YOUR FLIGHT!" Sarah asked Camila.

"Fine," Camila said without a trace of accent, dancing her fingers on the tablecloth like a smoker without a cigarette. Sarah sensed hostility from Camila — the intensity of the gaze, the pressed-together lips — but held out the possibility that she was wrong again.

"Camila's been living with an aunt in Miami since she was four," Michael said. "The traffic from the airport was torturous."

Camila was serious, wary.

The tuxedoed maître d' pored over the reservation book.

With slender, pearly fingertips, Camila brushed a strand

of hair out of her eye, as Sarah folded her own workman-like hands into fists under the table. The calloused writing finger. Camila's dimples could be Michael's, although if she passed them on the street she wouldn't recognize them. Sarah's shoulder ached, and she turned to face Camila at less of an angle, the lights of the city blinking beneath the skyscraper restaurant. Clouds were sparse; an F-16 returned home.

The restaurant was near empty; a man with his leg in a cast and cuts on his face occupied a corner seat.

Camila scoped out the restaurant, taking it in, then studied Sarah, until Sarah caught her. Camila looked away.

She wants me to disappear.

"Does your mother visit you in Miami?" Sarah asked.

"My company used to have an office in Miami," Michael said. He turned to Sarah. "Camila's going to be on a panel about affirmative action in newsrooms."

If Natalie Wood had been Latina, she would have looked like this.

A man with an unidentifiable chest wound took a seat. In Vietnam they were called chest-sucking wounds.

"What's your beat?" Michael asked Camila.

"Metro. Festivals, gentrification." Camila dabbed at a runny nose with Kleenex.

"The last time I was in Miami . . ." Michael said.

Placing her napkin on the table, Sarah looked for the ladies' room. The last time he was in Miami he came back with gifts from his employees. "Those receptions are a drag," he'd said.

"I want to know about you and my mother," Camila said to Michael.

Sarah returned the napkin to her lap.

"Why did you leave her?" Camila asked. Her eyes were piercing, haunted, her whole thin body rigid with accusation.

Sarah wanted to take her hand, but didn't.

"I TOLD YOU, I didn't leave Magdalena." Michael placed the bright green termite station in the cardboard box Sarah held open, glancing down at the gaping hole in the damp, dark earth from whence the trap came beside their yellow clapboard house. "You don't think prospective buyers will notice this?"

Why would Magdalena tell Camila a different story? And why was Michael checking his BlackBerry every few seconds? Sarah needed to get Camila alone. She put the top on the box and headed toward the garage, past the FOR SALE sign thrust like a spear into a whirl of ivy, and pulled a Kleenex out of her pocket and picked up a used condom from the street curb. She deposited the condom in the garbage can in the garage, and moved back outside.

A burial procession moved slowly past, funeral signs perched on top of cars like little hats.

"I want a New Orleans–style jazz band when I die," she said.

"I want classical music." He snagged a weed with a nail-bitten hand as tall trees waved overhead. He pulled up a green plant, brown roots dangling.

"That's not a weed," she said. "If it were up to you, our yard would look like a military haircut."

A blue jay searched for a bird bath.

"Is it true male dogs' urine kills grass?" Sarah asked.

"There's no dog in my novel, but I changed its sex and breed to protect Random's privacy."

"But the husband in your novel is a former Latin American Peace Corps volunteer who became a businessman."

"Is Camila going to let Magdalena know she contacted you?"

"I told her to."

His cell phone rang, the strains of "Yankee Doodle Dandy" hopping through summer air.

"I'M FEELING BETTER," Camila said, looking lost in an oversized sweater and happy to see Michael. A line was forming in front of the receptionist in the emergency room as the man at the head of the line searched his pockets for an insurance card. On a television in the corner, two talk show guests came to blows about whether the war in Iraq replicated the mistakes of Vietnam.

"You were right to call," Michael said to Camila.

Paintings of ships on worried waves hung from the walls, and the hospital newsletter on the coffee table showed pictures of aging donors.

"They think it's food poisoning," Camila said. "As soon as they bring my follow-up instructions we can go." She turned to Michael. "I know you didn't leave my mother." Taking a pack of Marlboros from her purse, she tapped out a cigarette. "I called her and told her I'd tracked you down." Shoving the cigarette back.

Someone knew how to find Magdalena.

"Why didn't you tell her before that you'd called him?" Sarah asked.

"My mother had told me that some doors are best left closed."

Sarah had never known so many reluctant conversationalists. Michael had grown increasingly nervous.

Camila looked up at the ceiling as if stretching her neck, then back down again. "When she learned about her pregnancy, she was desperate — it would have been a scandal if anyone found out, and her father would have disowned her." She looked over her shoulder.

"Why didn't she tell me she was pregnant?" Michael asked.

"She didn't want you to marry her because she was pregnant," Camila said. She shook her head. "It's hard to believe, but apparently sex was a big deal in those days."

"A *very* big deal." Michael leaned his forehead into his hands.

Great.

"What was nothing to us was huge to them," Michael said. He sat up. "Not that it was nothing to me," he said to Camila. He glanced at Sarah.

"What did Magdalena do when she found out she was pregnant?" Sarah asked Camila.

A nurse holding a clipboard entered the waiting area. "Camila Rodriguez?"

Camila stood and looked at Michael, as if for reassurance, before following the nurse.

Sarah could feel her blood pressure rise, although it was supposed to be a silent symptom.

"DO YOU THINK Camila really had to rush back to the conference?" Sarah asked, the back of the den couch sagging behind her. "Why don't you call her?"

On television, Nazis burned books.

"I TOLD MICHAEL I was going to tai chi," Sarah said to Jacob. It was hard to restrain from fingering the thick, textured paint of the orange and yellow painting on the gallery wall, the blue one just as seductive. Michael was having lunch with Camila; Sarah hadn't been invited.

"Michael doesn't like abstract art," she said.

"I brought you a book," Jacob said.

"I love DeLillo," she said. His style not unlike this art.

"Do you ever think it would be nice to have the appropriate music wafting out of a book as you read?"

"How's your novel coming?"

"I've cleaned out three closets. Did you finish preparing for your lecture?"

"The slides are being finalized as we speak." He winked and moved toward Sarah as she walked backward. She hit a wall, and he kept coming.

A flock of children poured into the room as a guard slowly circled a sculpture and moved closer, bending over for a better look. *If I'd had a child, I would have taken her to the museum every Saturday, after which she'd have to race off with Michael to basketball. That would have been okay.*

Taking Sarah's arm, Jacob led her out of the room.

"I would feel better about this," she said, "if we were planning a surprise party for Michael."

"YOU'RE SHITTIN' ME!" Michael said, pacing with the phone to his ear, as Sarah rearranged boots at the bottom of the hall closet. He was talking with Camila, who'd refused to chat with Sarah when Sarah answered the phone. "You're shittin' me!" Michael walked back in her direction and sank into the brown leather armchair. It sounded as if Camila had engaged in another inquisitional phone conversation with Magdalena.

Following Random to the French doors, Sarah let him

out, stepping into the enveloping warmth of the sun on the deck as Random shopped for the right spot in the yard. The rain had stopped, and leafy branches of the birch rose and fell, breathing, as a bee investigated purple blooms and a robin dug for worms.

Hiram entered from the side yard, calves bulging beneath his post office blue bermudas, the brown pouch slapping his thigh as he handed Sarah the mail. "I thought I'd find you back here."

Random yawned.

"'They're taking my route away from me.'" Hiram said. "It's the higher-ups, not my doing. They're giving it to a woman. Michelle's okay. They're adding four blocks — it'll be the worst route in the city. I'm going to half-commercial, half-residential, so the distances are short. You can go into a store when it snows."

He hiked up his bag. "The tips aren't as good." White lines spoked from the corners of blue eyes on his leathered face. He nodded his head toward the gray house behind them. "Mrs. Reynolds never gave me anything." He turned to go. "The higher-ups do things for no reason." He disappeared around the corner of the house.

"Good luck!" Sarah said.

Michael came up behind her. "When she found out she was pregnant," he said, "Magdalena joined the guerrillas."

· · ·

THE METAL JAWS clamped down on her left breast, pressing like a waffle iron, as Sarah looked away from the mammogram technician.

Camila was vague about what happened after Magdalena joined the guerrillas, Sarah supposed because Magdalena had been vague. The generalized vagueness was infuriating. Was Magdalena on a cross-country throat-slashing rampage, or sitting grandmother-style on a rocking chair knitting.

"Hold your breath!" the technician shouted from behind the curtain.

This is what drowning would feel like. There should be art to look at.

"Breathe," the pink-smocked technician said, returning to rearrange Sarah's breasts for the next photo.

Camila was so young when she was sent to live with her aunt in Miami, three or four. Had she inherited her mother's bloodthirsty ways? "She's thinking of moving to Boston," Michael had said. The metal plate scraped Sarah's collarbone on its way to smash her breast.

A year and a half ago, Sarah had received a phone call from Rachel, stuck in a hospital with an undiagnosed malady, thirty minutes after Sarah had visited her. *A doctor left a pamphlet on my bed saying that most people who get this syndrome have cancer. She dropped it there and ran out of the room.* Rachel had a family history of cancer, which terrified her. Sarah had been busy and hadn't rushed to Rachel's bedside.

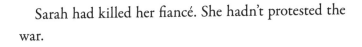

Sarah had killed her fiancé. She hadn't protested the war.

"COME WITH ME to meet Eric," Sarah said to Rachel. The middle rung of the surgeon's waiting-room chair cut into Sarah's back as she held Rachel's coat and tote bag.

"How'd you find him?" Rachel asked, continuing to fill out the lengthy medical history.

"On the Internet, not him, his sister. When I told her who I was, she said she'd like to meet me, and Providence is only about an hour and a half away. She sounded odd."

A woman sitting across from them was wearing an obvious wig, and Sarah stifled an impulse to jump up and hug her, but she knew her gusts of well-intentioned effusiveness could startle and give rise to deep misunderstanding.

Rachel rejected support groups. Various interpretations of this could be made.

"Why don't you get information from Camila?" Rachel asked.

"She's not talking."

"Camila's the one to watch," Rachel said.

Sarah tried not to look out the dizzying twenty-first-story window; below, a crane operator toyed with the universe.

"I never get this question about changes in bowel movements," Rachel said. "*Of course* things change when you vary your diet. What does a normal bowel movement look like? Do you take the average of the various kinds?"

Sarah studied a woman reading *Parents* magazine. No one was talking, and Sarah was sure they could learn things. It was too bad she couldn't write about Rachel. That would be exploitive.

She'd met Rachel when she lived in D.C. One morning Sarah climbed aboard a bus heading to M Street, and saw a scowling woman reading *Thousand Years of Women's Poetry*.

Rachel tried to change one of her answers, the pencil eraser spreading dark streaks across the paper.

OUT THE WINDOW, birch trees bent toward the house as Sarah sat on the black love seat, the list on her lap.

Mexico — an hour earlier
London — six hours ahead
Venezuela — an hour ahead
Argentina — two hours ahead
Brazil — an hour ahead
Colombia — same
Portugal — five hours ahead
China — twelve hours ahead
Japan — fourteen hours ahead
Singapore — twelve hours ahead
Thailand — eleven hours ahead
Spain — six hours ahead

Some numbers off because of daylight savings.

"You, too," Michael said from Chile.

"The good thing about having a spouse that travels," a friend had told Sarah, "is that you become independent. The bad thing is that you become independent."

Sarah glanced at *TV Guide*. Larry King was interviewing his ex-wives.

SHE LURCHED INTO the left lane, edging in front of a speeding red Corvette. Coins, pens, and pieces of Kleenex rolled around the floor of Sarah's Volvo, which she intended to clean up as soon as she wasn't late.

The green exit sign appeared in a timely fashion. Sarah had never watched the TV show about Providence, which might have given her some indication of what to expect when she met Eric's sister, Simone. Simone.

"I remember asking for Simone de Beauvoir's *Second Sex* in a bookstore in Ireland in the sixties," she said to Rachel, who sat rigidly in the passenger seat observing the wild flight of scenery. Rachel liked to drive.

"They told me it was 'banned,'" Sarah said. "Only you know how they pronounce 'banned' as if it were 'bunned,' and I had to ask the clerk three times what she was saying because I'd never heard of a book being banned."

Her white car hurtled down the exit ramp and came to a sudden stop.

• • •

SIMONE SAID SHE KNEW about Michael from Eric's letters, and knew they'd been close. They were competitive, Simone said, sizing Sarah up. Then something happened, Simone said, eyeing Sarah. Did Sarah know anything?

Simone seemed to think Michael was to blame for something. She knew about Magdalena and Camila.

"I'd like Eric's contact information," Sarah said.

"Eric's dead," Simone said.

"HE'S BEEN DEAD for years," Sarah told Michael. Simone didn't know how it happened. The vein at Michael's temple jumping.

The authorities claimed not to know what transpired, only that Eric had been shot. The letters might hold a clue to his death, but Simone hadn't given them to Sarah, only part of one because it talked a lot about Michael. A bead of sweat on his forehead.

Dear Simone,

Two weeks ago I was bitten by a rat, and had to get rabies shots in my stomach, and this, believe me, is not something you want to do. I had to take a bus every day to the comfy city office of the Peace Corps doctor. We have to give him monthly stool samples, so he can check for parasites, and once Michael dragged a huge worm out of some horse shit and put it in his stool specimen, and suddenly notices from the doctor were appearing on bulletin boards all over the country — "I must speak with Michael Bernino immediately! This is a matter of the greatest urgency!" When Michael did meet with him, Michael played it out, asked if he was going to die . . .

I guess I did have a sort of crush on Magdalena, which distinguishes me in no way from every other male in a 500-mile radius. There was a night not too long ago when it looked like I might have a shot, but Michael seems to have a lock; she's nuts about him, although it's hard to know what he's thinking since we mostly talk politics, music (thanks for the Janis Joplin), sports, books (thanks for the Frantz Fanon). I don't sense she's thrilled when he and I set off on one of our cross-country horseback treks. Que te vaya bien, she always says, in that husky voice, eyes lowered. Magdalena's the kind of person who seems to be winking when she isn't.

Did I tell you about the time Michael "delivered" a baby? We'd gone to a meeting up in the mountains and were on the way home when we stopped off at the campesino equivalent of a bar (a shack where they sell beer and aguardiente and have a generator to play music) with Mauricio and some other guys.

We were there for several hours and got pretty loaded, and, after a while, a little boy ran in and said his mother was about to give birth, that we had to rush over because the baby was coming — the assumption was that since we were North Americans we must know how to do everything, and all the focus was on Michael, probably because he was tallest. He said he didn't know anything about delivering babies, but a small crowd had gathered and they were relentless.

He remembered he had a copy of the Development Handbook in his saddlebag — a thick book we were given in training that talked about things like how to make bricks, how to grow stuff in your garden — and the last four pages of the book had illustrations of how to deliver a baby, step one, step two, etc.

"Boil some water," Michael said, because that was the first thing that flew into his head, and he went to his saddlebag to get the manual and began to read. "I need something to cut the cord," he announced professorily, "and some clean sheets." He kept studying the manual and was sweating bullets, but the pregnant woman was there by the side of the road and told him not to worry, she'd already had five children. She squatted, and the baby popped out.

Attempting to gain some measure of control, Michael, reading from the manual, grabbed two pieces of rawhide from his saddlebag and tied off the umbilical cord, then cut it with his knife. The book said it was important to keep the afterbirth and take it to a doctor so it could be checked for diseases so Michael put it in a burlap bag and tied it to his saddle horn. Then the woman cooked us breakfast.

Two hours later, when Michael and I had been riding in the heat, the afterbirth stunk to high heaven, and Michael untied the burlap bag from his saddle horn and slung it down a gorge.

Michael can be a pain in the ass.

. . . if you could see the way people here look at you with their eyes full of hope . . . There are pictures of JFK in huts all over the countryside . . .

Michael put the letter down.

"WE SPENT ALL WEEKEND getting ready for the appointment," Sarah said.

"Popcorn?" Jacob asked as he held the movie theater door open. Sarah shook her head, and they proceeded to the ticket line, where a purple-haired, eyebrow-pierced waif waited ahead of them. She couldn't be going to the same movie.

"After we cleaned and dusted," Sarah said, "I moved everything extraneous into the closets or basement, and hid all my prescription medicines. We placed the best books on the coffee table, a variety of choices, appealing to diverse tastes. There's a yellow-orange cover on *Dancing with Cuba,* which adds a spot of color to the living room."

An ambulance drove by the theater with a siren like the one in the Anne Frank movie.

"I straightened the piles in my study, and, again, there were choices to be made about which books to favor or hide. I placed *Campaign Finance Reform* on top.

"For the bedroom, we have a special duvet cover that Random hasn't soiled which we bring out for these occasions, and I let it hang long on the door side where it's more visible, and barely covering the top of the sheet on the other side which you don't see unless you walk around the bed.

"We put flowers in the living room and the bedroom. We want to put a note by the ones in the living room saying that we always have flowers in the living room, that this is not contrived, but it's not true that we have them in the bedroom. Michael buys carnations, which are pedestrian, but I don't tell him because he's the one who drove to get them. He wouldn't come to this movie, by the way, so thanks. The subtitles, black and white. It's not true that he wouldn't come, but we would have to see some other movies first and then he'd be off traveling and the movie would leave town."

Sarah turned to look behind them, and felt a sense of satisfaction at the superiority of their position in line relative to the hordes that now crowded the theater.

"Two," Jacob said to the woman behind the window.

He took the tickets and they climbed the oddly designed carpet on the stairs.

"We don't allow ourselves to go to the bathroom the last half hour before prospective buyers arrive," Sarah said, "to avoid the possibility of odors. Those cover-up sprays may be worse than what they're trying to cover up, but there's a vanilla one I like.

"We spent two days getting the house ready, and ten minutes before they were to arrive we scooped Random up and got in the car and drove halfway down the block so we could observe. The realtor arrived with only a minute to spare, and twenty minutes later the couple pulled into the driveway in a black Audi.

"It's important to know the make of the car, apparently," Sarah said as they reached the second floor and headed toward the far entrance of the tunneled building, "so you know if they can afford the house or are engaging in a hobby."

They entered the small viewing room, and Jacob looked questioningly at Sarah, who selected seats two-thirds of the way from the screen on the right side.

"Michael usually sits on the aisle because of his legs," she said, "but I can do either way."

Jacob plopped down in the interior seat.

"But the couple was in and out of the house in less than five minutes," Sarah said, sitting in the aisle seat, luxuriating in a stretched leg. Her arm scratched against the built-in cup holder, and when two large women sat down in front of them, Sarah experimented with looking to the left of the head of the left one or looking between the two heads; to the left worked fine.

"After they left we went back inside the house and

collapsed in the living room, which looked so beautiful, unable to get over our shock that anyone wouldn't want to linger in this perfect environment, smelling faintly of vanilla. The sun from the garden was streaming through the French doors, the red painting above the white sofa had never looked so brilliant, the molding and sculptured mantel had never looked more regal under the tall ceilings. It was then that I noticed, in a far corner on the oriental rug by the Chinese vase, that Random had deposited a small heap of poop. It was practically still steaming."

The couple behind them raised their voices. "I thought *you* turned it off," he said.

"Do we need to go back?" she asked.

"Michael was deeply affected by the news of Eric's death," Sarah said. "I can tell by how hard he's ignoring it.

"He won't go to a shrink because he's afraid someone from his company will see him. He doesn't believe in them, and has refused to go back to the marriage counselor. Sometimes you have to wait for something awful to happen to find out who Michael is." She looked over her shoulder. "I've invited Camila to a family dinner. Rachel thinks she's a time bomb." Sarah had heard Michael whispering on the phone.

The woman in front of Sarah and Jacob was on her cell: "Attacking Afghanistan made sense, but *this* . . ."

Sarah asked about Lennie, who was doing okay, Jacob

said. Jacob was going to San Francisco to lecture and why didn't Sarah come with him? She made a joke, which made him angry. The squall passed. She thought.

"What's happening with your novel?" Jacob asked.

"There's great drama in the last third, but middles are a struggle. I've given the woman comfortable financial circumstances, but that's a mistake, because critics hate characters who aren't working-class or poorer." People born rich were born blind. She and Michael were going blind slowly.

"No one escapes tragedy."

"People don't believe that. Nothing inflames people more than someone else's wealth."

Her foot slid across something crunchy on the floor. "Systemic change is called for."

"What are you doing to advance systemic change?" The lights dimmed, and instructions about fire exits and cell phones appeared.

"Campaign finance reform is the most important thing, but I can't think how to write a bosom-heaving, bodice-ripping book about campaign finance reform, so I'll write a light novel and try to find a way to slip it in."

"Good luck."

Blinding, flashing lights and piercing, shrieking sound effects crashed around them as the previews began, and Sarah closed her eyes against the painful overload of stimulation.

Jacob kissed the back of her neck.

Married people should remember the back of the neck.

ANNIVERSARY CARD to Sarah from Michael —

Illustration of Eloise, children's book character, yawning: "I hate Hate HATE boring."

"MICHAEL WAS BEATEN to within an inch of his life," Sarah said to Camila. Sarah shifted in the uncomfortable dining room chair inherited from her mother; one bulb of the chandelier was out. She knew things Camila didn't; Camila couldn't catch up.

Pale blue shadow covered Camila's lids in an unnecessary emphasis on the eyes, and she wore tapered black pants and a silver cashmere sweater and silver earrings. She moved her chair closer to Michael.

"It wasn't that bad," he said. "Eric saw worse."

The dining room floor slanted; you could run downhill from the southeast corner.

"You know I don't like asparagus," Michael whispered to Sarah as he reached for the potatoes.

"I would cook more often," Sarah said to Michael's mother, "but . . ." Sarah rolled her eyes at Michael.

"You used to be an excellent cook," Sarah's mother said, dicing her asparagus.

"Who's Eric?" Lisa asked.

"He was Michael's best friend in the Peace Corps," Michael's father said, wearing a red and white checked shirt like something Raymond would wear on television. "A good-looking young fella. Remember the time we took you out to eat at that steak house? When we came to visit in San Diego during your training?"

"What do you think of California?" Sarah's father asked. "The people . . ."

Bartholomew squealed when Michael kicked him.

Lisa was watching Camila. She looked at Sarah, then back at Camila.

"Camila, tell Lisa about the column you wrote on the Cuban community in Miami," Michael said.

"Are they plotting a coup?" Lisa asked. "Is our government supporting it? Because, if you like, you could come with us to the demonstration on Sunday."

"Something's rubbing against my foot," Sarah's mother said.

"Camila's leaving Sunday," Sarah said.

"The following Sunday," Camila said. "I was able to tack some vacation time onto my trip." She looked at Michael.

"Great!" he said.

"Great!" Sarah said.

Lisa did the ping-pong look between Sarah and Camila.

"What happened to you?" Camila asked Michael. "About the beating. Was my mother there?"

"We should meet for lunch someday," Sarah said to Camila. If she could get her alone . . .

"We'll all go," Michael said.

Lisa slipped Random a carrot.

"Where did you get your shirt?" Camila asked Lisa.

"The farmers' market."

"Great color," Camila said.

"Have you had time to read my poem?" Sarah asked her father. "The one about Mother's Day?"

"I haven't seen any African Americans up here," Camila said.

Sarah turned to Michael. "Do you want to explain Boston, or should I?"

"Are the people in your country short?" Michael's mother asked Camila.

Sarah wanted to touch Camila, but didn't.

"They have an extraordinary culture," Michael said. "A rich, centuries-old mix of Spanish, Indian, and African influences, you wouldn't believe how cosmopolitan the capital is, and don't forget Camila is American."

Camila gazed with doe-eyed gratitude at her protector. She, too, had moved her untouched asparagus to a far corner of the plate.

Lisa leaned over. "Cool tattoo," she said, of the small orchid on Camila's ankle.

"Random is looking askance at me," Sarah's mother said.

• • •

SARAH CLIMBED INTO the roller coaster beside Rachel and sat on the ancient, wooden seat. Michael, Lisa, and Camila squeezed in behind them.

Sarah pulled the flimsy steel handlebar close.

"This is great," Rachel said.

"We haven't started," Sarah said.

Rachel put an arm around her, and Sarah turned to look at Michael, with his arms around Lisa and Camila.

"Here," Sarah said, handing Rachel a scarf. "Put this on." She helped her knot it under her chin, a fluttering of synthetic hair flowering at the forehead.

The rest of the passengers climbed aboard, and the unshaven attendant stopped chatting with an acquaintance at a neighboring ride, and approached the rusted mechanical gear, which began to pull and push, groaning.

The train moved forward, inching up a gradual but lengthy incline, chugging with apparent effort. As they neared the top of the steel hill, the smog-filled horizon came into view, and Sarah tried to remember if there were lightning anecdotes. A billboard moved toward them, and she wished it was the Coppertone ad of her childhood — the cute, curly-haired, goldi-locked girl with the puppy — instead of a plug for *I Want to Be a Hilton.*

She closed her eyes and gripped the bar. As their car crested the summit, it began to feel lighter, move faster, and it was flying, flying dowhill with incredible speed and power; *it's not centrifugal force, what is this feeling, the rush of wind pushing your face behind your ears, the thunderous white noise punctuated by screams, the top of your body threatening to leap out of the car, your connection to the seat a slivery thread, I'm going to die.*

Michael laughed demonically.

Rachel was silent.

Camila had placed her hand on the top of Sarah and Rachel's seat, and Sarah felt a fingernail stab in the back.

SARAH PRESSED HER NOSE against the shoe store window as a leashed Random tried to pull Michael on ahead.

"You should get some of those," Michael said, pointing to a pair of slender black Manolo Blahniks.

"Let's go in," she said.

He looked at his watch.

"Camila won't be there for a half hour," she said. Camila had selected the restaurant and the time for their lunch, requiring Sarah to cancel an appointment.

"Are you sure they allow dogs?" he asked.

"It's French."

Michael picked up Random and followed Sarah into the store, where two young female clerks greeted their only customers.

"Do you have Birkenstocks?" Sarah asked.

The straight-haired clerk led her to the other end of the small shop.

"Oooh, what an ADORABLE dog!" the curly-haired clerk said to Michael, who waited by the door. She was buxom, with a blemished face.

He beamed.

"What's her name?" Curly Hair asked.

"The Birkenstocks are here," Straight Hair said to Sarah.

"His name — it's a he," Michael said, "is Random."

"Handsome?"

"Random."

She leaned over and stroked Random.

Sarah eyed the sandals, glancing over her shoulder from time to time. She picked up a brown shoe. "Do you have this in black?"

Straight Hair headed toward the stockroom, as Sarah plopped down on an orange chair.

"Size seven," Sarah called after her. A box of peds lay on the counter, and a planeload of flag-draped coffins snuck onto the television in the corner.

Curly Hair fondled Random. "How old is Randy?"

"Random. Eleven."

"He seems younger."

"Yes," Michael said. "He's athletic, well-coordinated."

"I'm dying to have a dog," Curly Hair said.

"You *should* have a dog."

"My landlord won't let me. He's a jerk."

"He *is* a jerk."

"I wish *you* were my landlord," she giggled, chucking

Random under the chin as he recoiled. Random had responded warmly to Camila's affection, and Sarah had two feelings about that.

"I guess I'll have to move," the clerk said.

Sarah scanned a table of pointy high-heeled shoes.

"Be sure to check the pet policy," Michael said.

"What street do you live on?" Curly Hair asked.

"Tory."

"Oh, my God, I LOVE that street!"

Michael beamed. He hugged all acquaintances when greeting them; he'd gotten into the habit in Latin America, he'd said, couldn't stop.

"I could check and see if there are apartments available in the building on our block," he said. "I know the owner. Are you looking for a one-bedroom?"

Straight Hair returned from the stockroom carrying three boxes of shoes. "This is all we have."

"Yes. One bedroom."

Sarah opened boxes.

"I'll give you my card," Michael said, shifting Random to his left arm and groping in his pocket with his right hand.

"Oh, my gosh!" Curly Hair said, looking at his card. "I didn't know I was talking to a PRESIDENT!"

Michael smiled modestly.

Sarah closed boxes. "I need black. Thanks very much." She rose and headed for the door, past an armless, hairless manikin modeling clear plastic sandals.

"There you are!" Michael said to Sarah, with high-pitched enthusiasm.

"Camila should be at the restaurant now," Sarah said.

Curly Hair slunk away, pocketing Michael's card.

Sarah and Michael left the store, and Michael returned Random-on-his-leash to the sidewalk, where Random raced down the street as if the groomer was chasing him. Water streamed from tin buckets of flowers placed in front of a florist, and a car had a honking fit. Michael whistled as he looked in store windows.

"SOME PEOPLE WERE convinced Peace Corps volunteers were CIA," Michael said, loosening the tie Camila had admired.

Clouds moved across blue sky with a rapidity which promised action. Random was tied to Michael's white, wrought-iron chair, and the river was still, its pudding-skin surface marred by only the occasional bubble.

Camila leaned forward and placed her elbow on the rusted table, resting her chin on her hands; the table shifted slightly. She wore a sheer turquoise blouse with a lacy camisole underneath. Was it style or seduction? The eyes could be Magdalena's or Michael's, same with the cheekbones. The eyes were riveted on Michael.

"You have no idea how weird it was for North Americans to be living in the slums," Michael said. "Many of us tall and blue-eyed." He glanced at Camila, who winked.

The black waitress handed them plastic-coated menus.

"Thank you!" Camila said with enthusiasm, smiling warmly at the black woman. She put the menu aside to listen to Michael, pulling her chair closer, landing on Sarah's toe.

Sarah gasped in pain as Camila lifted off of her.

"Keep in mind this was the sixties," Michael said.

Sarah caught her breath. "That was when they had a rigorous screening process, and it was difficult to get into the Peace Corps," she said to Camila.

"There was a battery of tests," Michael said, "including psychological tests."

"Michael almost didn't pass because the shrink thought he was too competitive," Sarah said. Michael competed with people who didn't know they were playing.

Camila watched Michael.

"There was a blond guy in our group," Michael said, "and he noticed that people began showing up when he took his shower — it was from an elevated steel drum that had collected rain water; you'd pull on it with a rope to tip it. He couldn't figure out why so many people were coming — they sat on the ledge of a stone wall and watched — but it turned out they'd never seen blond pubic hair before, so he put up some plywood walls for privacy. People kept turning up, so he tore the walls down, letting people get their fill of the view, and after a couple of weeks they lost interest."

Camila chuckled.

"Have you decided?" the waitress asked.

Camila smiled apologetically at her.

"I'm not eligible for unemployment benefits," the man at the next table said to his companion. "Technically, I was an independent contractor."

"He was beheaded," a woman at another table said. "I heard the news driving over here."

The waitress took their orders, and Camila thanked her energetically.

Sarah rose. "The ladies' room is to the left of the bar," Sarah said to Camila.

Camila watched Michael.

THE DOORS OF ALL the stalls were closed, with a conversation in progress, and Sarah glanced in the mirror, where a pale, middle-aged woman bit her lip.

How would it be if she'd met her father at Camila's age. She'd think he was handsome.

Only one end of the conversation was audible. Sarah bent over and looked under the doors of the stalls; all but one were empty. The woman was talking on her cell phone. Sarah entered another stall and checked for sufficient toilet paper before locking the door. "Viagra sucks!" was scrawled on the door.

"I'm doing okay," the woman on the phone was saying.

The back of the door held no hook, and Sarah searched for a clean spot on the floor to park her purse, stepping with care.

"Actually, I'm not doing great," the woman said. "The gentleman to whom I hitched my star has been carted off to prison for bank fraud, and I'm consulting with lawyers to determine my liability."

The toilets were programmed to flush automatically, and Sarah's performed prematurely. A light spray.

SARAH SAT BETWEEN Michael and Camila.

"What happened next?" Camila asked, engaged.

If she'd just met him, Sarah would think her father was smart and well-mannered. She would think her father was perfect, and that her life would have been dramatically different if he'd been in it when she was young. That he could, still, save her life.

"When I first got there," Michael said, "I tried to organize meetings to get people to clear an area for a soccer field, but I was told I had to meet with Don Jose, a local politician who controlled the barrio. People paid him for favors. Don Jose hated me, and kept sending people to tell me I couldn't do anything without his approval, but I kept on, so they started threatening me. They told me I was going to be thrown out of the country, and threatened my landlord. One night I was coming home late — I'd been downtown, and had taken a bus, and when I got off three guys jumped me."

Sarah felt sick to her stomach although she'd heard the story before.

Camila's eyes widened.

"I showed up for work the next day," Michael said, "with an eye swollen shut, face black and blue, limping. I tried to blow it off, but the men I was working with were pissed. The next day, a couple of guys I knew came and got me, and asked me to come with them. We ended up at an old shed at the outskirts of the barrio, and they said they wanted me to identify somebody, and took me inside. There on the ground were the guys who'd assaulted me. My friends had beaten the bejesus out of them."

"Hot," the waitress said, placing their plates before them.

"Thank you!" Camila said.

"No one bothered me after that," Michael said.

Sarah started to speak, but was drowned out by Camila. "Awful!" Camila rested a hand on his wrist.

"ON THE OTHER HAND, we might cut you open and sew you right back up," the lean, athletic, white-haired, white-jacketed surgeon said to Rachel. Three rows of black-framed certificates and awards hung grim-faced behind him. Sarah squinted, and they disappeared; rabbits jumping out of hats replaced them. An oriental rug, mahogany desk, and tall windows framing air.

"If there's nothing we can do," the surgeon continued.

"We might cut you open and sew you right back up," Sarah scribbled in Rachel's spiral notebook. "If there's nothing . . ." *I'm not the world's best note-taker. Rachel's friend Barbara is better at this.*

"Under that scenario," the surgeon said, "you could go home the next day. Cancer grows faster after an operation, so we don't want to operate unless we're sure we can get 99 percent of it." His hand drifted toward the computer on the desk; his fingers tapped, edging closer to the keyboard.

Sarah drew frantic circles on the tablet to get the ink in the ballpoint pen flowing again.

Rachel sat next to her, her wooden chair closest to the doctor, a long list of questions on yellow lined paper drooping from her lap. "What would happen if I discontinued the chemo?"

"You'd feel worse than you feel on the chemo," he said.

Rachel was silent.

"If she had the major operation," Sarah said, "how long would she be in the hospital?"

"Around five days," the doctor said.

Rachel looked out the window.

"And would she be able to climb stairs?" Sarah asked. "She has stairs in her house, which she'd like to stay in."

Rachel continued to look out the window.

"She's just renovated the house," Sarah said. "The carpet is Larsen, from the Design Center, the floors are Brazilian cherry, an antique wardrobe, a built-in desk, Louis Quinze chairs, cherry cabinets in the kitchen.

"On the desk are pictures of her brothers, nieces, and

nephews — that's from Thanksgiving — and a picture of Rachel and her brother when they were three and four. And, of course, Tara's new baby."

"Stairs will be fine," the doctor said.

"What happens if I don't have the operation?" Rachel asked.

"The tumor will strangle your bowels."

Pulling a dull pencil out of her purse to replace the pen, Sarah pushed past the folded letter from Eric, and her purse landed on the floor with a thud. Rachel and the doctor turned to stare at her, as she bent over the note book. ". . . strangle your bowels," she wrote.

Rubber gloves lay next to the steel sink. Small packets of antiseptic cleanser.

SARAH PICKED THROUGH cards, receipts, and papers strewn among coins on Michael's bowfront dresser. *Luis Tirado, Presidente, Inversiones Iberios. S.A. Phung Thi, Ministry of Finance, Socialist Republic of Vietnam. Bank of America, withdrawal from checking, $100.* Phone messages from his chief financial officer, an employee in Argentina, his doctor, the cycling shop, and three from Camila. Sarah studied the dates and times on the pink message slips from Camila.

"What are you doing?" Michael said.

"I was going to raise the shade and saw the message from your doctor."

"He called with my cholesterol numbers."

"What are they?"

"I don't remember. Good, he said."

Sarah, who could recite her numbers from the past six years, sat on the bed near the spot on the white comforter where Random slept. No odd people, ambulances, or sirens had made their way into the room.

"What did Camila want?" Sarah asked.

"Just checking in."

"Three times in fifteen minutes?"

"She's a kid, making up for lost time." He sat on the bed and began taking off his work shoes.

She wasn't a kid.

He removed his other shoe. "She's pursuing the possibility of moving to Boston, and I gave her some tips. Do you know she's wanted to be a journalist since she was ten? She's been keeping a journal since she was nine; I think she wrote instead of talked. I don't sense she has a lot of friends. She has a wonderful, innate curiosity."

"Why hadn't you told me about your friends beating up the guys that beat you, the part you told Camila at lunch?"

Carrying his shoes over to the closet, he sat down in the gray chair.

"Tell me something you've never told anyone," Sarah said.

Michael looked as if he was going to say something, but didn't. Standing, he took off his tie, and walked over to the closet again, hanging the tie neatly on the rack. He stroked the tie, patted it, then closed the door. He examined the door. "Eric joined the guerrillas."

Sarah was still.

"He swore me to secrecy." Michael returned to the chair and sat down, leaning back.

Where to start.

"Does his sister know?"

"I don't know if he was able to write her then. Or call. I never heard from him after he left. We weren't on the best of terms at the end." He rubbed his temples. "It was before Magdalena disappeared, so they must have stayed in touch." He started unbuttoning his shirt, then paused. "I tried to stop him." He began unbuttoning furiously. "It's my fault."

When Michael was a child, he'd walked with his mother into a service station just as a display of oil cans toppled noisily to the floor. *Did I do that?*

What else did Michael know.

Sarah tried to picture it, Eric joining the guerrillas.

She thought about Marx saying religion was the opiate of the masses. Would Americans protest their government if they weren't so comforted?

SARAH HAD BEEN on the Internet, and learned things. Were they true?

She'd learned that, in spite of idealistic beginnings, the

guerrillas had begun producing and distributing cocaine to raise money (stimulated, Michael said, by the American appetite for drugs). And that the guerrillas had, increasingly, been augmenting their funds by kidnapping for ransom.

How long a ride had Eric and Magdalena taken.

How had it marked Camila. Conditions that would wreak havoc on the psyche.

SARAH DROVE BACK to see Eric's sister alone. Rachel hadn't made up her mind about having the operation.

Through some mean streets.

Parking was difficult and involved edging closer than was wise to a fire hydrant.

She stepped over sidewalk cracks and breaking mothers' backs.

Simone's house looked older, more paint-chipped than Sarah remembered. A tall young man met her at the door; dark curly hair and a large gap-toothed smile, above an unbuttoned flower-splattered shirt. He held a newspaper and tried to fold it one-handed as he opened the screened door and extended his other hand. "I'm Eric."

Sarah was motionless.

"My son." Simone came up behind him.

Sarah and Simone sat in uncomfortable iron chairs in the small backyard. An aging beech tree edged the patio, and nodding blue hydrangeas bordered the house.

Tortoise shell combs restrained Simone's thick hair, and a stain marked the collar of her black and white polka dot blouse. Sarah listened as Simone spoke about her work at the food bank. That was the sort of work Sarah should be doing.

"I know Eric joined the guerrillas," Sarah said.

Simone tapped her thumb on the chair.

"I'd be interested in what else you know about Magdalena," Sarah said. "And the child. Camila has been in touch with us; we know Michael's her father."

Simone looked across the fence.

"I know Magdalena joined the guerrillas, too," Sarah said.

"Eric told her where he was going when he left," Simone said. "It was in a letter. He went with a man they'd met one night when they got lost near her father's ranch. Eric had given Magdalena the man's contact information, and that's how they ended up in the same place when Magdalena decided to go."

"What can you tell me about Camila," Sarah said. Unable to imagine being born in a guerrilla camp.

Simone looked across the fence again, and paused, trying to recall, or something else. "Eric wrote about a hammock he made for Magdalena and Camila, out of hemp. When Camila was a baby, Magdalena would carry her around in a sort of pouch hanging from her neck. That's all I know."

"Edvard Munch Smith, COME HOME THIS MINUTE!" a woman shouted from the next yard.

"I'm COMING!" a young boy answered.

A slow-moving blimp carried an ad for an illegible product.

Simone had been sitting with one leg folded under her and switched legs. "Magdalena's father was kidnapped, by another band of rebels. Eric and Magdalena found out and were going to rescue him. That's the last I heard from Eric."

"I'm taking off, Mom!" Eric called from the porch.

SARAH TOLD MICHAEL.

"It's my fault," he said. Oil cans rolling.

"Do you think Camila's okay?" Sarah asked.

"What do you mean?"

"Psychologically."

"Of course."

When the counselor had given Sarah and Michael the Minnesota Multiphasic, or whatever that psychological test was called, it indicated that Michael was more impressionable than Sarah.

THE DOCK AT Long Wharf grew distant as the schooner inched away. Going for a "sail" on a sizable motorized boat in Boston Harbor was a touristy thing to do.

At the bow of the boat, Camila and Michael were laughing; occasionally Michael pointed at something with explanation, and Camila seemed to be telling amusing anecdotes.

Other passengers spread about, chatting, drinking, gawking.

The crew — college students on vacation? — attended to sails, food, drink. Boat traffic in the harbor evidenced appealing variety — yachts, rowboats, ships, fishing vessels, day sailors, trawlers, catamarans, cigarette boats — weren't those illegal? There was no evidence of port security.

Presuming it contained life vests, Sarah sat on a footlocker and observed the passing scenery. She turned her book — *Overcoming Loneliness in Everyday Life* — facedown on her lap. It was hard to tell if the boat was moving at all, so slow was its progress. *Are we moving, do we exist?*

Seagulls searched for garbage, skyscrapers leaping in the background. Harbor islands slipped past, and Sarah imagined their stories. Lovers hidden behind scrubby brush. Escaped slaves. A craggy mound that would make an excellent Alcatraz. Rare species of birds inhabiting the last hospitable speck of land on the planet.

A woman behind her with young children seemed to be a teacher, pointing out various sites, keeping Johnny from falling overboard, leaning down and putting an arm around Susie to hear her softly spoken question. Teachers, nurses, and police should be paid more. Sarah's intellectual friends criticized the CIA, the FBI, and the military, but didn't send their bright sons and daughters to work there.

The lure of prestige and high salaries. *We have the infra-structure we deserve.*

"Having a good time?" a young crew member fresh from adjusting sails asked.

"How long have you worked here?" Sarah asked.

"This is my first day. It's the first week for all of us."

"I'm going to the head," Michael said, passing.

"Excuse me," Sarah said to the young man, leaving to join Camila at the bow. Camila was uphill and upwind, scanning the harbor.

"Nice, isn't it?" Sarah said, holding the railing to leverage against the boat's tilts.

Sipping her drink, which looked to be scotch, Camila turned back to the horizon.

"This sort of thing must be gorgeous in Miami," Sarah said.

Camila nodded.

"Is there someone special in your life there?" Sarah asked.

Camila shrugged. "You know how it is, all the good ones taken."

"A beautiful young woman . . ."

"I'm kind of seeing someone," Camila said. "A friend's father."

"Married?"

Camila passed her tongue in front of her teeth, just as the boat heeled dramatically in the wake of a gigantic, fast-moving freighter, and Sarah tried to retain her footing as

Camila slid toward her, spilling her sloshing drink along the way, but Camila landed on Sarah with such force that Sarah was thrown backward, losing her balance, and falling halfway across the railing, which she gripped with one hand while the other flailed, trying to find it. Camila's weight kept pressing into her, and Sarah could feel herself losing the battle, when she heard Michael's voice.

"Hey!" He grabbed Sarah and yanked her back until she was grounded on deck.

"YOU'RE CRAZY," Michael said to Sarah, turning left onto their street. "Why would Camila try to push you overboard?"

WHEN SHE FINISHED reading Eric's letter, Camila looked up at Sarah. They sat on a green wooden bench at Harvard's JFK Park; someone had written EAT MORE PEACHES! with chalk on the sidewalk. Leaves sprinkled on grass. Trees of varying types, as if Noah had selected two of each, appeared sporadically.

"I thought you'd want to read it," Sarah said, "because it talks about Magdalena." And meeting with Camila alone might yield some answers.

Wearing soft leather boots with two-inch heels, flared slacks, and a silk scarf, Camila looked out across the grassy expanse. Sarah liked the way she dressed. She liked *her,* although she'd hoped not to, although Camila had given her more than enough reason not to. Perhaps because she seemed truly motherless, as if there were a genuine opening. Michael always said Sarah forgave prematurely.

When Sarah had arrived at the park, Camila was stooped on the grass feeding bread crumbs to the birds but stood abruptly and wiped her hands when she saw Sarah, the stiffness returning.

Two men exiting the university building strode past Sarah and Camila. "You can impose an analytic structure on the problem," one said to the other.

"Did you ever get the sense from your mother that she wanted to reunite with Michael?" Sarah asked.

Camila surveyed her lap.

"Let's walk," Sarah said.

A bent, gray-haired woman with a slow-moving, stiff, Irish wolfhound approached from the other direction, and the wolfhound and Random socialized before the humans moved on.

Camila watched a dark-skinned woman walking toward them. "Hello!" Camila said, smiling big, as the woman passed.

"I think it's a good thing Eric did," Camila said, "going off with the guerrillas. I would have done the same thing. Maybe I will!" She clenched her fist.

"What's your earliest memory of your mother?" Sarah asked.

"A picture, my aunt showed me a picture of her on horseback, she had long black hair. And she wrote letters. Sometimes she drew pictures or cartoons on them, she would include a joke.

"She used to call, too, about once a month, very lighthearted. I don't know what there was to be lighthearted about."

Sarah unwound from the leash.

"When I turned eighteen," Camila said, "I told her not to call me again. What kind of mother abandons a child?"

Random sniffed too close to a sleeping homeless woman before Sarah restrained him.

What kind of woman abandons a child before she's conceived.

"When do you and Michael move into your new apartment?" Camila asked.

Sarah clicked open her ringing cell phone, and put it to her ear.

"When I got back to my office after the meeting," Michael said, "I had a phone message. It was from Magdalena."

SARAH'S CAR PANTED at a stoplight. Wait until Jacob finds out.

Pictures of houses for sale covered a realty window,

and a man with an armful of cleaning shifted from one foot to the other in front of the funeral home.

In the lane next to Sarah, an unshaven, weather-beaten man in overalls sat in a pickup, and his sizable, tattoed forearm emerged from the window to adjust the side-view mirror, as Sarah clicked her doors locked. The truck driver leaned forward to turn up his radio and listened intently. It was NPR.

BOOKS LINED JACOB'S new rented apartment, warmed by lamps at varying heights as designers recommend. Was this one of those buildings that specialized in the newly separated?

He didn't mean to kiss her at the movie; it was an accident as he was leaning over. The back of the neck an erogenous zone.

Nina Simone grieved through speakers, and unopened moving boxes pouted in a corner.

"What did Magdalena say to Michael?" Jacob called from the kitchen, where he was cooking risotto.

"He hasn't called back." Sarah picked up Marie Howe. "I don't talk with my old boyfriends, kind of a professional courtesy." A Marie Howe poem had saved her the last time she'd felt writing was a waste of time.

Sarah returned the book to the shelf. A Habitat for Humanity T-shirt lay crumpled on a chair.

She studied the Elizabeth Murray prints, then walked past the dining room, where two places were set, into the kitchen.

A large butcher knife lay on a cutting board next to a knife sharpener.

"Did you see *Proof of Life*?" she asked.

"We saw it together."

A skateboard leaned against a wall in the corner. "I don't I ?" the ked.

"He doesn't make eye contact."

"Does he blame his mother?"

"He blames anyone who doesn't love his music."

Lisa liked alternative, underground groups that no one had heard of although they had fans everywhere.

Jacob squatted in front of the oak cabinet he was building, wood shavings beneath his boot, and drew his finger across a dovetail joint. The smell of sawdust, the ultimate aphrodisiac.

"Johanna wants me to come back," he said.

"Has she ended it with the Cirque du Soleil guy?"

He raised his eyebrows, stood. Reached for wine.

She waited to see if there was more.

He was silent.

"You're a terrific dad," she said.

She plopped down on a stool at the island. "This isn't an island, really, more of a peninsula."

Jacob approached the stove and turned up the heat, as

she twirled on the stool. "Is there something about you I wouldn't like if I knew it?" she asked. "Do you pick your toes?"

"Yes, and last week I canceled a meeting with AIDS activists to go to a Red Sox game."

"It was postponed, right?"

He shook his head. "They had to leave town."

"What you don't like about me," Sarah said, "is that I don't seem to listen, and I make wisecracks when things are serious."

He picked up the spoon and stirred. Someday he's going to leave.

"How's the move coming?" he asked.

"One more trash night before we go."

"Is your apartment ready?"

"The contractor says we'll only have to stay in a hotel for a couple of days."

Jacob spoke about the difficulties of fund-raising, the cost of gas, NASCAR culture, a dental experience.

Sarah looked out the window. "I've been considering epigraphs. You know, the quotes that authors put at the beginning of their books."

"I'm not an ignoramus."

"I was wondering why authors don't write their own epigraphs, instead of quoting someone else; they're writers, aren't they? Why turn over such an important job to a stranger?

"I was thinking T. S. Eliot's 'The whole earth is our hospital' could be good, but it's not quite what I'm getting at."

Jacob picked up a taro chip and bit into it. "We're searching for an epigraph for your book?" He looked up at the ceiling, then nodded. "Stendhal: 'Politics is a millstone hung on the neck of literature.'"

"But you see," Sarah said, "I would want to edit it. I might take out the 'hung' as being unnecessary."

He kissed her. Not an accident.

SARAH WIPED A floret of vomit off the edge of Jacob's leather boat shoe with toilet paper.

He sat slumped over on a wooden stool, chin in hands, in his ochre bathroom.

"You couldn't help it," she said, depositing the paper in the john and flushing. "It wasn't your food, I'm fine."

"There's a bug going around."

That was a stupid thing people said.

Sarah removed a washcloth from a rack and held it under cold running water at the sink, then folded it lengthwise and wiped his forehead. "They do this in the movies."

She returned the washcloth, opening it out to dry, and dried her hands on the towel. "Don't you want to lie down?"

He shook his head. "It's going to happen again soon."

His face was pale, the dark eyes glistening, and a corner of his hair squashed where she'd pressed the cool cloth.

Sarah sat on the edge of the tub. The black and white tile was chipped in a number of places. A Gary Trudeau cartoon hung above the toilet, and although she couldn't read the caption, she smiled anyway, a Pavlovian response. The toilet was Kohler, and had flushed with elegant discretion.

"When I was little," she said, "I wanted to be a movie star or a nurse. I liked Cherry Ames better than Nancy Drew, and Debbie Reynolds better than Elizabeth Taylor; now I would reverse things."

"How's the movie star thing coming?" Jacob asked.

"I'm furious with the paparazzi. The only good thing is being able to raise money for charity and entertaining the troops." Jonathan had joined the Marines at the height of the Vietnam War; he thought his mother was overreacting. Michael had gone reluctantly, which hadn't prevented his being shot in the leg and shoulder. He'd had a skin cancer removed recently, and almost passed out at the familiar scent of burning flesh. It was something they had in common, Vietnam. The shadow of a small country. It made you feel lonely around people who didn't get it.

"I wanted to be a panther when I was a kid," Jacob said.

"I saw the track trophies in your bedroom. Oh — Rachel doesn't want to meet you."

"I love Rachel. If you die under mysterious circumstances, by the way, I'll tell everyone it was Camila. Think Glenn Close in *Fatal Attraction*. 'I will not be *ignored*.'"

He shifted his weight. "I'm feigning illness to get your attention. I'm jealous of Rachel."

"I do like to feel needed."

"Does Michael need you?" He jumped to his feet and leaned over the toilet bowl, as Sarah placed a hand on his back, turning her head away, trying to breathe through her mouth.

IT WAS TWELVE hours between his time and her time, and he called at his night and her morning.

"Beijing is fascinating," Michael said. "We saw Tiananmen Square."

"The plumber said we made an excellent choice on the new toilet," Sarah said.

"We had dinner with the ambassador."

"It's the most problem-free toilet made."

"The meeting with the premier was at the People's Council building — huge and breathtakingly beautiful. I've never seen anything like it. Gorgeous, enormous murals at either end of the hall, around fifty yards long and fifteen feet high, multicolored, painted with incredible detail, traditional Chinese landscapes — jagged mountains, mist, deep gorges. Storks. The color of the room itself was a kind of muted gold, beautiful crystal chandeliers dropped from the ceiling, everything very tasteful, like Versailles in a Chinese motif, and big comfortable chairs, the only red in the room, but a pretty, subtle red, with white doilies, but nothing prissy about them. I wish they'd given us just fifteen minutes after the meeting to look at the murals."

"It shouldn't keep running the way our other toilet did, and flushes well. The plumber wadded up all kinds of paper and tried it, with excellent results, and he said if we use Scott paper there will be fewer clogging incidents."

MICHAEL AND CAMILA pushed through from the rain, slamming umbrellas shut, as Sarah held the door open. Michael's desire to take Camila to the zoo ("A father should take his child to the zoo") had not been deterred by Camila's age, his still-packed suitcase, or the weather forecast. He hadn't called Magdalena back, unless he was keeping it from Sarah.

"Great!" Michael said, setting his black-handled umbrella down, and bending to remove his Adidas. "We had two hours of sun before the storm hit."

Camila, looking as radiant as he, dark hair plastered and dripping, face polished by rain, leaned a pink umbrella against the Japanese-inspired wallpaper. "I didn't know they had ocelots." She oversmiled.

"They have rhinoceros beetles," Michael said. "I'd like to take Camila to the aquarium, too, but there isn't time before she leaves."

Camila seemed to have inherited Michael's fascination with the underwater universe, particularly if it was Caribbean, and she'd listened to Michael's scuba-diving stories with rapt attention.

"Random pooped five times today," Sarah said. "A record, I think."

Moving his shoes out of the way, Michael wiggled his toes in their multicolored socks. "I'm going to show Camila our Web site, she's interested in the company's growth."

"He's promised to come see me in Miami in a couple of weeks," Camila said.

"You shouldn't have given Random popcorn last night," Sarah said, as Michael ran up the creaking stairs.

The sofa was deep for her back; Sarah stared at the potted palm across the room. She'd explained to Michael that palms were predictable, that they should get an exotic plant. The elegance of its slender spokes undeniable. The red carnations he'd bought before his trip stared back at her.

Instead of beginning a new chapter, Sarah doodled. A ficus tree. The profile of a man. Jacob had an interesting profile. *I wonder if I have any e-mail.* She headed upstairs, past the rip in the wallpaper.

"I don't know what happened," she heard Michael say as she approached his study.

"Here, let me try," Camila said, taking the computer mouse and beginning a series of rapid-fire movements. They sat shoulder to shoulder, backs to Sarah. Pictures of

Michael fly-fishing, sailing, biking, on his Harley, carrying a shotgun, and wearing scuba gear hung on the walls. Cycling shoes rested in a corner next to a couple of briefcases, and pottery and malachite from Latin America and ivory from Asia spread out among the (all nonfiction) books on the shelves. The humidor he'd asked her to buy him for Christmas. She'd been permitted to pick the wood — rosewood or walnut — and had selected rosewood, but now it looked orange, garish. A glass case with cycling trophies. Upbeat Latin music.

"There," Camila said, dabbing at her nose with Kleenex. "I'm allergic to mold."

"What did you do?" Michael asked.

"I'll show you." She passed the mouse back to him. "Click on System Preferences." A lock of her hair falling on his shoulder.

Easing out of the room, Sarah walked barefoot across the wooden floor, lingering on the warm spot where Random had taken his most recent nap.

CAMILA AND SARAH reached the passenger door of Michael's car at the same moment; Sarah walked to the back door and entered as Camila moved into the front seat.

After arranging Camila's luggage in the trunk, Michael got into the driver's seat and adjusted the rearview mirror, before backing down the driveway, forcing a pedestrian to run for cover.

The empty seat beside Sarah stretched. It was too bad the airport didn't allow dogs.

Michael braked for cyclists crossing the street, and Camila checked for her plane ticket in her purse. "Are you going to call my mother back?" she asked Michael, who'd scattered another group of pedestrians.

"I need to think this through," he said, stopping for another group of cyclists. Michael's phobia about addressing the situation verged on the pathologic, but, at this juncture, Sarah was happy for it, and keeping her happy could be one reason he hesitated.

Wearing a black pin-striped suit, Camila clutched copies of the *New York Times, El Mercurio,* and *El Pais.* She had a column for her own paper due the next day, and Sarah hoped she wasn't anxious. *Why am I feeling compassion for this woman?*

Pausing at the stoplight, Michael flicked a speck of dust from the dashboard; he kept a fluffy feather duster in the trunk. Someone had scrawled "the war" under STOP on the octagonal red sign.

SARAH STOOD ASIDE while Michael took Camila's suitcase — black with a gargantuan purple plastic orchid — out of the trunk of the car and set it on the curb in front of the airport. She hoped the orchid was for identification purposes.

"Wait here," Michael said. "I'll park."

Sarah and Camila stepped onto the sidewalk as Michael pulled away, inserting himself aggressively into the traffic flow.

Camila searched in her purse, and a plastic pill bottle fell to the ground, bouncing lightly, and she bent over in a rush and grabbed it, swooping the bottle away and back into her purse before Sarah had a chance for a good look.

"Do you have a headache?" Sarah asked.

Shaking her head, Camila turned to watch other travelers. Security officials held poles with mirrors under cars.

Camila shifted her purse from the left arm to her right. "It's only Xanax," she said. "They belong to my aunt. I have trouble sleeping sometimes, or before a big interview, something like that. She gave me some for the trip." Glancing over her shoulder. "I would appreciate it if you didn't mention this to Michael."

A redcap dragged an overloaded, squeaking cart between them.

Camila cleared her throat and fixed Sarah in her gaze. "I want him to like me." The aquamarine eyes of a five-year-old.

A hot and cold young woman. When was she being manipulative, when was she being sincere, were they the same?

Eventually, Sarah forgave everyone but Hitler.

"Let's go inside," Sarah said.

They headed for the door. "Wait," Camila said. She stopped, and fished the pill bottle out of her handbag, holding it out to Sarah. "I want you to see I was telling the truth about what's in here."

Sarah covered the bottle with her hand and pushed it back into Camila's purse.

AS THEY APPROACHED the security gate, Camila stood in line between Michael and Sarah, and looked at Michael, who put his arms around her; the tension slipped from her body. She bent toward Sarah, who returned her embrace.

Sarah felt every bone. As with Lisa, she tried for distance. A borrowed child. *You're going to protect yourself right into loneliness,* Michael had said. *They're all borrowed.*

The bumper sticker on the car in front of them was illegible, as Sarah and Michael idled, stuck in the tunnel. When Sarah was a child, she'd read the cod liver oil bottle while eating breakfast.

"Did you hear that Romania is banning women over sixty from sunbathing topless?" she asked. "They say the 'Ugly Show' is distracting tourists."

"You're not sixty."

"That's not the point." Traffic began to move.

"Something needs to be done," Sarah said, "to bring attention to the issue."

"Whatever it is, please don't do it near my office."

Traffic came to a halt. "That was a good visit, wouldn't you say?" Michael said. "With Camila?"

A moment. "Yes."

"She seems to be a nice young woman," he said.

"Yes."

"I hope she follows up on her plans to move to Boston."

Traffic picked up, light at the end.

Nothing should be inferred.

LETTER TO SARAH —

Madrid

. . . The two deepest regrets of my life are that I didn't meet you earlier, and that we didn't have children of our own. With respect to the first, perhaps fate knew better than we when the best time would be for us to meet. With respect to the second, I am consumed with sorrow, a deep pain I buried away somewhere, because that was a decision, as you know, that I made. I think I was still shell shocked from my divorce, some great, nameless fear . . . and I don't know how to say I'm sorry for something which has a meaning far greater than anything we could have imagined at the time, or will ever know.

Something comes over me when we're apart. Let me tell you about the meetings . . .
Michael

THE BEEPING SOUNDS on Rachel's heart monitor were steady and consistent, not going berserk the way they did on television. Sarah sat on a backless stool next to the hospital bed, as Rachel flipped through her Rolodex and reached for the phone.

"Sharon? Rachel!

"Great! But I need to reschedule the meeting with Jefferson. I'm going to be out of town for a few days."

In the hall, a doctor was speaking with a young woman wearing a white jacket. "I'm happy for you to accompany me on rounds, but you must think before you speak. Ask me any question you like once we're back in my office, but if we're with a patient, you must consider how something could be interpreted. For example, don't say, is it cancer?"

"Jefferson's a dolt," Rachel said, replacing the phone, and sinking deep into the pillows. "His firm provides 10 percent of my income." She looked at Sarah. "This isn't the end of Camila, you know."

She looked at Sarah closely. "Have I seen that blouse? I like it; it's a different shade of black."

"This morning when I went out to get the newspaper," Sarah said, "I realized I'd worn it yesterday, and was embarrassed that the plainclothesman watching our house saw me wearing the same thing two days in a row."

"Watching the house?"

"A man at the company got fired. Michael didn't do it, it was someone else, but there were threats." Sarah stood and walked over to a plant on the windowsill, picking up the card. "The guy was operating a male escort service out of his office." She read the card, then put it back on the sill. "In the movies, people living in the houses being guarded bring sandwiches and things to the car of the people watching the house, and I did that the first time, but it started feeling like pressure. What kind of sandwiches should I make, etcetera."

"Have I been at the house when it's been watched?" Rachel asked.

Sarah thought about it. "The night I burned the salmon." She paced. "Sometimes they make me feel safer, but other times, the idea that grown men think there need to be guards to keep someone from killing me scares the . . ." She sat down by the IV dripping into Rachel's arm. "What time's the operation?"

"Between ten and one tomorrow. They have to fit me in." She looked out the window; the venetian blinds were askew. It was a gray day, or maybe the buildings were gray.

Rachel's briefcase stood next to a chair, and a couple of

manila file folders slid toward her foot on the faded blue bedspread. Sarah spun on her stool.

"Would you pray for me?" Rachel asked.

"Of course," Sarah said, coming to a halt. Rachel looked out the window.

"Prayer works," Sarah said.

"Sometimes," Rachel said, not shifting her gaze from the tall tower on the medical campus.

Sarah had flirted with Buddhism, but missed Jesus and Hanukkah, knowing it, bore holes.

When Sarah prayed, she offered heartfelt thanks for Michael, Random, and the house; the house stood for many things, Michael and Random stood for themselves, and then she prayed fervently for Rachel and *all those in need,* slipping herself into the prayer anonymously.

An image of a plane on September 11 flashed before her. "Would you like to say the Lord's Prayer? We could say it together." She winced at the banality.

"The Twenty-third Psalm," Rachel said.

Sarah scooted her stool closer to the bed and took Rachel's hand; Rachel squeezed back.

"The Lord is my shepherd," Sarah said.

" . . . is my shepherd," Rachel said.

"How's it going, hon?" Janice, the nurse, said. She'd missed a button on her blouse.

"Will Dr. Garcia be stopping by?" Rachel asked.

Janice fluffed her pillow. "Let me know if you need anything."

"The Lord is my shepherd; I shall not . . ."

A squeaking steel cart piled high with linens pushed into the room, followed by a blue-jacketed male aide, who replaced towels in the bathroom.

"Could you tell Dr. Garcia I'd like to see him?" Rachel asked.

"I shall not want," Sarah said. "He maketh me to lie down . . ."

"Medicine!" Janice said. She held the little paper cup with the pills as Rachel swallowed them one by one with the water Janice had brought. Why were they sitting there watching her throat undulate as if it were theater?

Rachel nodded when she was done, and Janice put the cup down on the table-with-wheels before leaving, a tomato-colored stain on her hip pocket.

Sarah picked up speed and volume. "IN GREEN PASTURES; HE LEADETH ME BESIDE STILL WATERS. HE RESTORETH MY SOUL: HE LEADETH ME IN THE PATHS OF RIGHTEOUSNESS FOR HIS NAME'S SAKE. YEA THOUGH I WALK THROUGH THE VALLEY . . ."

"SEVEN DOLLARS," the red-uniformed hospital parking attendant said from behind her glass cage, an open paperback copy of *The Joy of Writing Sex* lying next to the cash register.

Sarah passed a bill through the car window. "Stephen Levine said we're afraid of death because we believe we were born."

The woman handed her change, pink nail polish chipped.

"As if there were beginnings and ends. Not understanding it's merely a change of form."

"Have a nice day," the woman said.

CLOSING THE room behind her, Sarah greeted Random halfheartedly, stepped over half-packed moving boxes, and crumbled on the couch. Lacking the energy to stand, she leaned across sofa pillows to reach the answering machine, pressed the button with her little finger, and turned up the volume.

"This is Harvard Book Store calling to say the book you ordered, *News of a Kidnapping*, by Gabriel García Márquez, has arrived. We'll hold it for three days." *beep*

She turned down the volume.

The click of someone who hung up. *beep*

"This is Susan at Island Realty. Thanks for your inquiry about homes in the Keys." *beep*

"Hi, Sarah, would you mind dropping by my house and picking up my palm pilot before you come to the hospital tomorrow?" *beep*

The afternoon sun magnified the coat of dust on the floor.

"Hello, Michael, it's Mom. Hello, Sarah, too. Just thought I'd check in since I haven't heard from you." *beep*

The cracks in the molding had deepened. Don't let the house collapse before the closing.

"This is Mighty Movers. Please call Erica to confirm the details of your move." *beep*

The click of the hang-up person again. *beep*

Was it Camila?

"Hi, Dad and Sarah, it's Lisa, calling to see how you're doing. Could you lend me some money until next week?" *beep*

"Hello there! This is Bob at Aloha Realty! Got your request for information about oceanfront condominiums on Kauai." *beep*

It used to be that Oahu was exotic enough; now you had to go to another island.

"Hello, hello . . . Hello . . . Sarah, are you there? . . . Let me know if the dry cleaning came back today, otherwise I'll have to buy another shirt for my trip. What a morning . . . Did you hear the weather report? I was thinking it might be interesting to find out how much apartments cost in La Jolla." *beep*

"This is Mary Potten, again, from collections, about your Visa bill." *beep*

"This message for Michael Bernino? Please call [a very long number]." *beep*

A low, husky female voice, probably a smoker, heavily accented. The phone number began with a country code.

Sarah stood and ran to the answering machine, almost tripping on the large box labeled GIFTS FROM MICHAEL'S PARENTS, frantically pushing buttons to skip over other messages to get to the last one. She played it again, grabbing a pen to scribble the phone number. There are moments that can change a life.

The message could be erased.

No criminal penalties, no political fallout

Sitting, she took a deep breath, cleared her throat. Dialed.

"Hola," the woman answered.

Sarah hung up.

AFTER REREADING THE paragraph in Eric's letter about Magdalena, Sarah looked over at Michael, slouched in the red chair.

"Do you think about her?"

"Who?"

Sarah pressed her lips together.

"I didn't used to."

Looking down at the thin-papered letter on her lap, Sarah ironed the wrinkles out with her hand. "You had a phone message today. On the machine."

• • •

THE RIGHT FRONT wheel of Rachel's wheelchair refused to revolve, like on a stuck grocery store cart, and Sarah had to half lift, half push the chair across the coral-colored hospital lobby. She examined the wheel again, which had strands of hair caught in it.

The operation had been brief. Opened and sewed her right back up.

"I'm perfectly capable of walking," Rachel said. Masses poured into the reception area, more coming in than going out, and the line for the help desk snaked through the room. People sat impassively on rows of metal chairs attached to the floor; a woman studied an Arabic-English dictionary, and a throng huddled around the YOU ARE HERE map.

Sarah parked Rachel in front of the floor-to-ceiling windows at the entrance. "I'll get the car; don't come out until I come in for you."

Rachel exuded disgust. "Will Barbara be there when I get home?"

Sarah nodded. "She's going to get you settled and make some supper."

"Did Michael call Magdalena?" Rachel asked.

"I'll find out tonight." It was hard to know whether she or Michael was most afraid.

"This place is badly organized," Rachel said. "The nurses' movements are inefficient. I've begun a flow chart."

Will I be like this.

Sarah walked up the gray concrete steps of the stairwell in the parking garage through vapors of urine, sweat, and mold.

She ascended the next flight, stepping over a puddle, was it level C? She pushed the heavy door open and looked out at rows of cars, nothing looked familiar. Aren't the Mini Coopers adorable. The door slammed shut behind her, and she walked up to the next level. "What did you do during the war?" the wall said.

After rolling Rachel to the curb, Sarah helped her into the front seat. Cars, trucks, and ambulances swirled around them, as uniformed persons tried to exert control, and tall buildings with many windows looked down on the scene.

"Is that my phone or yours?" Rachel asked. "I'm expecting a call about the conference."

SARAH OPENED THE passenger door and scooped a shivering Random out of the front seat. He'd been shaking since Schott Street, when the car turned onto a familiar route.

She carried him into the animal hospital and planted him on the floor, where he quaked. An invisible cat — eyes darting wildly in a darkened crate — snarled and hissed. A large golden retriever with a languidly swaying tail, like a branch in the breeze, observed the new arrival, and Random approached cautiously, sniffed, and joined in the tail-wagging. A puddle of pee, where fear had overcome a previous patient, sat in the middle of the pale linoleum floor.

Sarah leaned on the reception desk and indicated the glass cookie jar. "Would it be okay if I gave Random a treat?"

"Not until it's over."

The waiting area was half full. An Airedale terrier napped at the feet of an elderly woman, and a caged parrot rested on the lap of a middle-aged man. Two teen-aged boys clutched crated creatures, and a young woman stroked a restless kitten in her arms; an empty-handed, heavyset woman sat across from her.

Sarah perched next to the empty-handed woman. Ads for flea collars, heartworm protection, and pet insurance lined the walls, and tattered "missing" posters, with faded photographs like those pasted around the World Trade Center, littered the bulletin board. Stacks of pet food — the kind that's good for teeth, the kind that's good for allergies, the kind that's good for old age — stood on metal racks in the corner, and colorful Frisbees, squeaking toys, and balls danced next to the muzzles, cages, and leashes.

Sarah had taken to calling Camila from time to time, hanging up when she answered, because it made her feel safer to know Camila was still in Miami; she couldn't trust Michael to tell her things. There'd been no answer the times she'd called today.

A man walking a mixed-breed dog entered, and the

terrier strained against his leash and barked; the golden retriever wagged his tail, and Random jumped into Sarah's lap, observing intently, ready for the show. "The economy, stupid!" the parrot said.

Random trembled, and Sarah gave him a body massage, whispered sweet nothings. She did like to feel needed.

"How old is she?" the empty-handed woman asked the kitten stroker.

"Two months," the young woman said, shifting the kitten to the other shoulder in an attempt to achieve stasis.

"Mine's three," the older woman said. "*Cat Fancy* is an excellent magazine, you'll find it useful."

The young woman tried to calm the kitten.

"Dr. Whisker's food is the best," the older woman said.

The young woman tried kissing the kitten.

"They like to be scratched behind the ear," the older woman said. She stood and approached. "Do you mind?" The older woman bent over and scratched the kitten behind the ear, as the kitten took a clawed swipe at the woman and hissed. The woman returned to her seat.

"Random?" the whited-coated technician asked.

Sarah placed Random on the floor and stood, giving the leash a gentle tug, but Random plopped his rump down, dug in his heels, and resisted any forward motion. After sliding him a few inches, Sarah picked him up and followed the technician to the scales.

• • •

RANDOM PRETENDED NOT to notice that the vet had entered the examining room, staring determinedly in the opposite direction, willing the vet's nonexistence, as Sarah held him still on the stainless steel table. A chart on the wall showed pictures of various breeds with descriptions of their characteristics, not mentioning that bichons get cataracts, beagles howl, golden retrievers suffer hip dysplasia.

"Hello, Random," the vet said, petting Random with one hand and reading his file with the other. Random began wagging his tail wildly, having entered phase 2 — "I'll be so cute you couldn't possibly hurt me."

The vet, who had a dried yellow streak across his white jacket, put the file down, and felt the glands under Random's throat, around his rib cage, then took a thermometer from the shelf, "This isn't going to hurt," and inserted it gently into Random's backside. Random wagged his tail all the faster.

"I've *never* seen that," the vet said.

Will I be like this.

RANDOM RAN OUT of the building so fast Sarah felt a painful pull in the tendon in her arm. She placed the treats on the ground in the parking lot, and watched Random feast.

"How'd it go?" Jacob asked, the gray gravel crunching under his green and white running shoes.

"What are you doing here?"

"WHAT MATTERS MOST in the world to me — " Sarah said.

"How's everything?" the waitress asked.

"Fine," Sarah said, not making eye contact.

"Fine," Jacob said with a wave of his hand, watching Sarah.

He had well-shaped, elegant fingers, the kind that glided across piano keys.

"What I should say," Sarah said, "is, what mattered most to me twenty years ago — "

"Can I get you anything else?" the waitress asked.

Sarah and Jacob shook their heads.

"I read," Sarah said, "that the primary desire of all humans — "

"I can take this whenever you're ready," the waitress said, slapping the bill down on the table.

"If I had a restaurant," Sarah said, "I would have a button on the table you could press when you wanted the waiter — a little red light might go on — and the waiter would be forbidden from coming to the table unless the light was on."

Once Michael ate steak and drank beer listening to rock on the roof of a hotel in Saigon as mortars flashed around them.

A photograph of the employee of the month hung on the wall beside Jacob, and a woman in a booth behind them read a magazine with an ad for Christian cosmetics on the back.

"Michael's traveling," Sarah said. "When we were dating, he said he was afraid to leave on trips, afraid I wouldn't be there when he returned.

"The best was Sunday mornings. We'd sleep late, we'd . . ." she glanced at Jacob. "We'd have brunch at Avignon Freres. Have you been to Avignon Freres?"

He shook his head.

"Maybe it no longer exists."

"Where is he this time? What's he running from?"

She felt stimulated. "That's the first time you've said something negative about Michael."

"I let my guard down. I understand that the best strategy is to refrain from criticism, and that I'm to play the saint, but a sexy saint."

At the televised convention above the counter, a young brunette woman at the podium was speaking. "My father said, 'you're alive, and you're an American. That makes you the luckiest girl in the world.'"

"I was thinking about being dead," Sarah said. "And how the world will go on and fascinating things are going to happen and people will wear absurd clothes and sit on ridiculous furniture, and I was flattened by grief, not that I would miss it, because I've grown accustomed to that idea, but about the things that *won't* change, there will be war after war, people will go on killing each other into eternity, and I wanted to rush ahead and explain things and stop it."

"Have you considered antidepressants?" Jacob asked.

Sarah sat back in her chair. "There will be music."

"I love you," he said.

No.

"Do you want to know why?"

No, no.

"Remember when we were watching the Tour de France," he said, "and it was an incredibly exciting moment with Lance pulling ahead, and all that extraordinary countryside, and cyclists racing down the roadway, and you kept talking about the cows in the fields alongside the course frightened by the helicopters with the cameras in them, the blades of the helicopters stirring up that powerful wind digging deep, billowing waves in the tall grass and terrifying the cows, who kept running down the fields trying to get away from the helicopters, and the television commentators never mentioning the cows? I love that you watch the cows."

That was not the sort of thing Michael admired.

SARAH AND MICHAEL sat in front of the television, she with Stouffer's spinach soufflé (a side dish, but she ate it as an entrée), and he with Santa Fe rice and beans.

Pen marks covered the arms of Sarah's chair, sections of the *New York Times* were scattered on the floor, and everything else in the room was packed in labeled boxes. The white carnations Michael had bought stood unyielding on the dining room table.

The lush, soon-to-be-abandoned backyard looked longingly at them through the French doors. The beech tree named Alice, the Japanese maples. "I saw on the Weather Channel about a man who collects Japanese maples," Sarah said. "Isn't that the most wonderful thing to collect?" There were, of course, also, weeds.

Michael mixed his rice and beans. "Where were you this afternoon?"

"Random's checkup. And I ran into my friend Jacob; he's having horrible problems with his son."

Accompanied by the kind of music that tells you things are very scary indeed, the television anchor opened the nightly news listing the major stories — the Middle East, the political campaign, the rescue of a small girl who'd fallen into a manhole. The hard news had appeared on the Internet two days prior. Sarah had considered writing a blog, but you needed journalistic credentials, and she was out of synch; when Walter Mondale ran for president and said he would raise taxes, she thought it was a good thing because he was telling the truth, and when sweater-wearing Jimmy Carter told Americans they suffered from malaise, she could see it.

"How was your meeting this morning?" Sarah asked during the commercial (a man who thought he'd had Alzheimer's had something else altogether).

"Chávez is consolidating power in Venezuela," Michael said, "the acquisition in Chile is going through, the dollar's down in Brazil." Michael's Spanish fluency was useful (he'd tried to learn Portuguese — not so good), although he was a little vain about it in this country, always chatting up Latinos.

News of the political campaign was distressing. "How was your four o'clock meeting?" Sarah asked during the next commercial (a movie star made extra money pushing cell phones).

"Spain and Portugal are coordinating nicely, a dam ̶l̶ ̶ ̶ ̶ ̶ ̶ ̶i̶n̶ ̶C̶h̶i̶n̶a̶,̶ ̶S̶i̶n̶g̶a̶p̶o̶r̶e̶ ̶i̶s̶ ̶o̶n̶ ̶s̶c̶h̶e̶d̶u̶l̶e̶." Michael had cycled in Spain, fished in Portugal, admired the tidiness of Singapore, and been transformed by China. *If you haven't been, you can't understand.* Sarah seesawed between admiration and human rights concerns.

Sometimes there were crises at work, and Michael called her. He called her, too, when he had a written report to produce, and needed to procrastinate.

"And did you call Magdalena?" Sarah asked during the story about the little girl and the manhole.

Michael held up a finger, staring at the TV as if he needed to hear every word.

Eyes on the girl.

"DID HE CALL HER?" Lisa asked. Only a handful of people had straggled in to find seats at the bookstore's poetry reading.

Sarah nodded, shifting on the hard wooden chair, craning her neck to read titles on shelves.

"And?" Lisa asked.

"She wants to meet with him, but he didn't say he would." Out the window, a long line formed at Computer World.

"Why does she want to meet with him?"

"She said the matter was best handled in person."

"Do you think she wants to get back together with him?"

"Of course not."

"Is she still with the revolutionaries?"

"No, but she wouldn't talk about what she's done since, or when she left." A woman sitting a few seats away wore a button that said YEE HAW! IS NOT A FOREIGN POLICY.

"Going to this poetry reading was the stupidest idea you've had," Lisa said. "Worse than the time you sent me that newspaper clipping about singles night at the museum." She wore an A-line denim miniskirt with patchwork pockets, a purple tube top, and a green corduroy jacket with her yellow tights, black lace-up boots, and dangling sequin earrings.

Lisa had charmed Rachel when Rachel spent Thanksgiving with them, when Rachel had called Michael a curmudgeon, and he'd laughed with delight to be associated with such an interesting word. Later, Lisa complained that Rachel talked too much; Lisa didn't like to share. Once, years ago, Sarah and Michael had spoken openly about having a baby; Lisa felt it was a bad idea. Camila's exoticism must have overridden Lisa's jealousy.

"I thought you might meet a better class of men than the ones you find at bars," Sarah said to Lisa.

"Clubs, not bars, and clubs aren't what bars were when you and Dad were young. And how many people do you think I'll meet sitting next to my moth — stepmother?"

"I told you I'd sit in another row."

"The only people here are women, old women at that."

"It's possible I didn't think this through sufficiently," Sarah said.

On the podium, the glass of water stood expectantly.

Lisa turned to Sarah. "Camila's neck is short."

THE PILE OF CLOTHES on Rachel's bed dripped off the sides, chartreuse blouse spilling over V-necked sweater, black dress sliding across wool pants.

Rachel's wig had had a permanent. She'd come from a meeting and wore a suit with a gold necklace her mother had given her; her mother gave her things she could sell, how can a single woman make her way in this world? There were no flowers in Rachel's perfume.

An academic robe hung on a hanger from the top of the door.

The mountain of clothes on the bed called. "I thought I was here to help turn the mattress," Sarah said.

"Spring cleaning," Rachel said, picking through clothes.

The empty closet rolled its eyes. "It's Halloween," Sarah said.

"Ghosts, goblins," Rachel said. "What exactly is a goblin?" She took a yellow blouse from the top of the heap and handed it to Sarah. "You should wear color. Try this on."

She returned to the pile and pulled out a rose dress. "This would look good on Anne-Marie." She added it to several items folded on a chair. "I want my down coat to go to Barbara, and Marty can have the turquoise sweater."

Sarah sat down on a rocking chair, yellow blouse wrinkling on her lap. "I'm not doing this."

"Sophie likes the black skirt," Rachel said. "Did you know her parents belong to the Hemlock Society? Only it's not called that anymore, something else. They tell you how to take the Seconal, how many you have to swallow, in applesauce, I think, but then there's a bit about putting a plastic bag over your head, and I wouldn't be able to do that.

"So many methods leave a mess," Rachel continued, "a problem for the people who find you. I thought the best way would be in a running car in a garage, but I don't have a garage, and would have to borrow one from a friend. One needs help with this sort of thing,"

She turned to Sarah. "What do you think?"

Outside, a tiny bird perched on the window ledge, a tinier speck of food in its beak. Coming or going? Feathers like filigree.

Someone had thrust a broken red and white umbrella head first into a trash can.

Downstairs, Rachel's answering machine kept up a steady business.

"In the Netherlands and Switzerland," Rachel said, "they're more sensible about end-of-life issues."

Sarah balled up the yellow blouse and threw it back on the bed. "You said you'd go with me to the reading tonight. You never come anymore."

"Maybe it's because you can't stop babbling about whatever you've fastened on most recently with your in-finitesimally small attention span."

"You forgot Random's birthday," Sarah said.

"You spent three-fourths of our lunch last week talking about torture policies and prisoners of war when you knew I was going to get the results of my CAT scan that afternoon," Rachel said.

"No wonder you never got married!"

"You never returned my Jane Fonda workout book!"

"That was twenty years ago!"

Rachel took the yellow blouse, folding it lengthwise, and held it as she looked out the window. She placed the blouse across the pile on the chair and studied Sarah. "I wanted to buy some new clothes this weekend, and needed to make space."

Sarah's knees stopped shaking.

Rachel kicked off her heels, and approached the bed on stocking feet, pulling a tie-dyed shirt out of the pile. "Can you believe we wore these?"

Sarah stood. "I had earrings down to my boobs."

Walking to the bed, she stroked a black velvet blouse. "We could paint a bull fighter on it." She picked up a navy blue blazer and put it on.

"Add a tie and khaki pants," Rachel said, "and you could be a male suitably dressed for any occasion in the South."

Sarah drew one of Rachel's business cards out of the pocket, as Rachel took a piece of paper from the dresser and handed it to Sarah. It was a quote that sounded like don't hide your light under a bushel, and don't minimize your talent to keep people around you from feeling jealous.

"Write your damn book," Rachel said.

Sarah passed her thumb across the embossing on Rachel's card.

She glanced at the bed. "The dress to Anne-Marie, the coat to Barbara, the sweater to Marty, the skirt to Sophie."

Barbara had the garage.

SARAH LEANED BACK against the blond hotel headboard, as Michael stepped over piles of papers, books, boxes, and clothes in the cramped room. Random's suitcase filled the chair. Nondescript art hung on the walls, and the window didn't open, but you could tell the weather by what people were wearing.

Michael scooped out a hole on the floor and sat down with his *Financial Times*.

"Don't go see Magdalena," Sarah said, notes for her novel scattered beside her.

"I thought the contractor said we could move in Friday," he said. "Who's supposed to pay for this?"

"The electrician hasn't done his part, and that has to happen before the floors can be done, or vice versa."

"I thought that was the reason we didn't move in last week," Michael said.

"They painted the bedroom the wrong color."

"How can you get in him a couple"

"Ecru, oyster, bone . . ."

He waved his hands to make her stop and tore through his paper.

"What's Camila's role in this?" she asked.

Lisa's mother would have cried to get her way. Sarah rose and went to the minibar, the chemical-smelling carpet slightly damp on her bare feet. She reached behind the shelf with the intimacy kit for the chocolate chip cookies, hoping they weren't oatmeal cookies with raisins masquerading as chocolate chip, then stood and studied the card with the cable offerings. HBO, Showtime, Lifetime, ESPN, Weather, CNN, Al Jazeera, Headline News.

Random sniffed the carpet, then flipped over and rolled back and forth, legs dancing in the air.

"THEY JUST BLOW a little air into you, take a few pictures, and bam! It's done!" Sarah snapped her fingers.

"Nothing to it!" she said to Rachel. Sarah's own barium enema had been worse than a root canal.

The wooden bench on which they sat in the hospital basement waiting room was hard, perhaps to ease you into things. Rachel had already changed into the white gown with blue flowers on it, and Sarah tied it in back and took her street clothes and purse. Rachel grimaced as she shifted position; her distended abdomen made her look seven months pregnant, and she tried to bend toward the floor. "Could you tie my shoes?"

Sarah set Rachel's belongings on the bench, and knelt in front of her, tying her laces. "I feel like an apostle at the feet of the Lord."

"I'm a fraud," Rachel said.

"We all are." Sarah returned to the bench. "When do you get the results of the X-ray?"

"About a week." She checked her cell phone for messages. "I've taken on two new clients, which means things will be busy for a while, but they're my first biotech companies — it could open some things up." She'd stopped trying to give away her things.

Sarah stared at the linoleum floor, gray and yellow squares.

"When does Michael get back from Turkey?" Rachel asked. "How many times has Camila called?"

"Tonight. He doesn't tell me."

Another woman in a hospital gown stepped out of a changing room, clutching her clothes to her chest, scouring the room before taking a seat at the other end of the bench from a heavyset man reading a newspaper, knees flopped apart, his splayed legs revealing more than was necessary under the gown. A daughter helped a mother with a crossword puzzle, stroking her hair.

"My mother was in a nursing home for six years," Rachel said. "The last time I flew home to visit her, she asked me to stop by on the way from the airport to the hotel, but I needed to work out, and said I would see her later." But by then it was too late. Sarah could remember from the last time Rachel had told her.

"Rachel Sumac?" a young woman with a chart said. Rachel and Sarah stood. The woman with the chart blocked Sarah from following Rachel down the hall.

So many people talked about bright lights at the end of a tunnel, being greeted by loved ones who'd died, which was comforting, but there were scientists who said the lights are neurological phenomena in the brain, which sucked the comfort right out. Sarah crossed her legs and looked around the waiting room, rubbing her aching shoulder. She couldn't believe she'd forgotten to bring a book; *The Unprofessionals,* called "a masterpiece of comic despair" by its publisher, was edging nervously toward conclusion. Jayne Anne Phillips was quoted as saying "I read for allies and illumination." Here was an ally.

Sarah switched legs, crossing the right one over the left. What would she do if she didn't have Michael to come with her to scary medical appointments, if he was in town? To take Random for walks when she was sick, if he was in town and not in a meeting? *I have a wonderful husband. He calls me three times a day, and tells me he loves me. He writes me letters when he's out of town, and if I suggest something like going to a movie or taking a trip, he's enthusiastic, he's the most energetic person I know. I'm proud of him when we're with other people, he's kind to my mother. He's funny and smart and vital and sexy and works his tail off from morning until night so we can have a roof over our heads, and doesn't nag me to get a job that pays and is delighted when something good happens to me.*

The woman sitting on the bench with the sloppily positioned man picked up *Forbes* and began to read.

The hands on the large black wall clock stuck.

Rachel padded down the hall, and Sarah sprang to greet her. "That was quick."

"My phone," Rachel said, pointing to her vibrating purse on the pile of clothes on the bench.

Rachel sat on the seat and held the phone to her ear. "Great!" She held her hand over the phone and turned to Sarah. "That's the nurse at my doctor's office — she's gone to get him. They already have the results!"

SARAH ORDERED THE chicken satay, putting her menu down on the paper napkin and stainless steel fork. She turned to Michael beside her in the booth, then poked in her jeans pocket for Kleenex. Bubbles of black paint protruded from the wooden seats like pocks. One other patron, an elderly man, sat at a lonely table in the dusky restaurant.

The smiling (Thai, one assumed) waitress took orders.

Norma, sitting across from Sarah, nudged Brevard, her husband, and suggested spring rolls.

"Her second surgery's the day after tomorrow," Sarah said. "The first one showed outside the colon, this is inside."

Norma shook her ⁙⁙⁙⁙⁙⁙⁙⁙⁙ ⁙⁙⁙⁙⁙⁙

Michael had had three crises today.

Brevard ordered rice and tea and slapped the menu shut and handed it to the waitress, who asked if they wanted spring rolls. He shook his head. Norma told the waitress they wanted spring rolls.

It was a large restaurant to have so many empty seats. How could they make money? That was a thing she'd learned from Michael, to be always thinking *How can they make money?*

"Rachel's niece was supposed to come," Sarah said, "but the baby's sick."

Michael rubbed the small of Sarah's back with his thumb. Out the window, a flat, matted squirrel lay on the street.

Michael didn't know if he was going to see Magdalena; he'd told her he'd call at the end of the week.

Brevard asked Michael about the Hong Kong deal, Norma asked Sarah about *War Trash,* Brevard asked

Michael about fly-flishing, Sarah asked Norma if the living room rugs clashed.

"WHY DO WE have to get a new rug?" Michael asked, holding the glass store door open for Sarah.

"You heard her."

"She said the rugs were fine," Michael said. He was good about accompanying Sarah on these errands, and sometimes had better taste than she.

Sarah whooshed into the large store. "And we can trade in the Tabriz, don't mention that Random throws up on it." She looked at her watch. "Don't let me forget to call Rachel at 10:30."

The closing door shut out the rushing people and car sounds, but you could see them in the store's tall windows, like a silent film. Would they pull out black umbrellas and dance.

Piles of Persian, Tibetan, Indian, and Pakistani rugs arranged themselves in neat stacks according to size, and colorful carpets hung from the walls, the hangings more beautiful than the more accessible piles.

"Hello..." A young blonde with a British accent glided over, holding a coffee cup and wearing what looked like tennis whites.

"We're looking for something knockout gorgeous," Sarah said.

"What size?"

"What size are those?" Sarah asked, pointing toward a tall heap topped by an intricately designed rose carpet.

"Nine by twelve," the blonde said. She snapped her fingers, and two slight Tibetan men wearing navy blue Colonial Carpets T-shirts ran over to the mound of rugs and positioned themselves on either side.

The blonde snapped her fingers again, and the young men began lifting the large carpets one by heavy one, and rolling them back so the rug underneath would be visible.

"Let me know if something interests you," the blonde said.

The small men — hunched over and eyes averted — continued to pick up and pull the mammoth rugs.

"That one's nice!" Sarah blurted, bringing the labor to a halt, but Michael shook his head.

The blonde motioned for the men to begin again, and they bent, lifted, and tugged, walking backward and hoisting the rug over the mountain of previously rejected ones.

"We appreciate the work," Sarah said to the hauling men, who didn't seem to speak English.

"We *love* doing this," the blonde said. "It's our job!

"Would you like some coffee?" she asked Sarah and Michael, indicating a table across the room. "We have espresso, French roast, hazelnut, you name it."

The men moved rhythmically, toting their bale of rug. A sound like the crack of a whip.

AS SARAH AND MICHAEL drove back empty-handed, Michael's cell phone rang, and he took it out of his pocket and glanced at the number flashing on the screen. "I'll call back."

"Who?"

"Camila."

SARAH WALKED THROUGH the hotel corridor toward the lobby, past a conference room where gray-suited participants seated at white linen tablecloths gazed out the window, and a speaker pointed to a slide that said SEAMLESS PHASE TWO. In her previous life, Sarah had been a frequent panelist and presenter; everyone wanted to know how to get funding. Few would.

"Good morning." A brisk hotel employee nodded to Sarah as he passed. "How's Random?" A family with two children juggled suitcases and backpacks of varying sizes and colors, as Sarah moved past the concierge huddled over his phone, and deposited herself on the Corbusier-inspired leather couch.

People with briefcases and laptops waited in line at the registration desk. "It's behind the mayonnaise jar," a man said into his cell phone. "There are thirteen hostages," a woman said into her phone.

Visitors moved in and out of revolving glass doors to the street, pushing in slices of cold, and, diagonally across the room, a man wearing tattered clothes and worn shoes pulled his jacket tightly around him, fists thrust into his pockets, trying to calm his shivering. He kept a steady watch on the black-jacketed security guard, wire to his ear, who was chatting with a redhead holding a fishbowl.

A newspaper tossed on the chair next to Sarah showed a picture of a tiger with a newborn cub. *I wonder if the mother's thinking,* "When can I go back to the office?"

Reaching for the phone in her purse, she opened the tiny red leather address book, found the number, and punched it in.

"Camila? . . . Great. And you? . . ." Sarah exhaled relief that she'd gotten the friendly Camila instead of the other one. It was the first time Sarah had called without hanging up; she had another agenda. "I'm sorry. How long had you been together? . . . He's a jerk. I know it feels awful . . . Well, among other things, I've been divorced . . . I joined a support group, got a shrink, read self-help books, but, as my mother had told me, the only cure was the next man."

What would become of her if Michael left her? She could have lunch with a different friend every day, but that was Chinese food — during her divorce, Sarah had calculated that it took five lunches with friends to equal one hour of emotional intimacy with a spouse. She wouldn't have the energy to have as many lunches as it would take to stave off loneliness.

Random had taught her that there was nothing humiliating about trying to avoid loneliness; he was a very secure, confident, independent dog, but hated to be alone, proving it was preference, not need — we're pack animals.

"Fine, he's in Australia, a fourteen-hour difference, and has written me a long letter, he said. Beautiful views of the harbor. You must have a pretty view . . . I'd love to, I might do that someday." So mercurial, this woman. "I was wondering if you could give me your aunt's phone number." The aunt would unlock Camila's secrets.

Camila didn't care. About anything.

SARAH HAD MOVED to a bench by the river.

On the next bench, a young man and woman sat smashed together at the end, using a fourth of the space. Geese swam with a knowing air.

"Of course he says 'I love you, too' when I tell him I love him," Sarah had said to the counselor. "What else can you say?"

"You'd be surprised," the counselor had said.

The coxswain barked orders to the gliding rowers, and a helicopter circled overhead. Yellow leaves littered the banks of the racing river. Picking up the script she'd written for her conversation, Sarah read it over, mouthing words.

She held the phone to her ear.

"Amelia Silva? . . . My name is Sarah, I'm married to Camila's father, Michael."

Sarah couldn't balance the purse, script, and phone, and the script slid from her lap to the ground.

"Hello? . . . We enjoyed visiting with Camila when she was here, a lovely young woman. I'd love to learn more about her."

A panting jogger passed, holding a hand to his heart.

The jogger seemed to falter.

"Yes, I also enjoyed a visit with Simone, the sister of Eric Mariner, a young man who was in the . . . movement   with your sister." A tiny pause. "I bet Magdalena mentioned him to you?"

The jogger was nowhere to be seen in the tall grass.

"Then you know about his tragic death . . . During the attempt to rescue Magdalena's father — your father — that's what we assumed." It was difficult to tell whether the siren was ambulance or fire engine.

"We don't know anything else, is there something else? . . . But we thought the rebels killed him, isn't that what happened? . . . Please don't hang up . . ."

Sarah stared at the small metal phone before clicking it shut.

She gazed out at the gray river, sometimes brown, sometimes green, sometimes brilliantly blue. Sometimes glass, sometimes opaque, sometimes heavy with the image of clouds.

• • •

"I'M GOING TO visit Rachel," Sarah said, hugging her knees to her chest. She sat on the floor of the hospital elevator, one of those long elevators with doors at both ends, which had been stuck for seventeen and a half minutes. The resident in his white jacket stared at the door, gripping *How to Write a Novel,* and another doctor staggered under the weight of the paperwork she was carrying.

"Rachel's had an ileostomy," Sarah said, "and has a pouch outside her abdomen. She believes the procedure will be reversed when she's better." *I'm glad it's not me.*

A woman wearing a shower cap and lying on a bed that had been rolled into the elevator groaned. "I wish this had happened after my operation."

"Is the operation necessary?" a man in a dark suit carrying a briefcase asked.

"I have to work nights at the grocery store to pay my mortgage," the nurse said.

The green-jacketed attendant who'd rolled in the shower cap lady fiddled with his cell phone, which had a camera and an alarm clock, while a long-legged, long-haired brunette wearing an Armani suit and dragging a Charlton Pharmaceuticals suitcase on wheels smiled and checked her makeup.

"I graduated from nursing school three weeks ago," the nurse said. "Yesterday they made me supervisor."

"I haven't slept in three days," the resident said. "I'm performing surgery."

"Here," the drug company model said, passing the

resident a handful of plastic-wrapped pills. "If you like," she said, "you can give a lecture about them in Paris, all expenses paid."

"I'm interested in research," he said.

"That, too," the drug model said.

"I have this lump on my arm," Sarah said to the doctor, as the patient in the bed moaned.

"I could give you a shot," the nurse said to the patient, "but we're out."

"I was misdiagnosed," the patient said.

"Don't get sick during a Red Sox game," the doctor said.

"Do you think they heard our screams?" Sarah asked.

The janitor with his gray mop stood next to his gray pail in the corner. "I'm moving to Canada."

"CANADIAN AUTHORITIES REPORT that they cannot accommodate the number of U.S. citizens who want to immigrate," CNN said. The TV stood on a box surrounded by other boxes in a den painted the wrong shade of green; the paint smell was strong, and plaster dust had settled in for the ages.

Sarah sat cross-legged on the floor, poring through stacks of books she'd removed from boxes. "Camila's aunt didn't want to talk with me, although I don't think she was angry, but maybe scared."

Michael stood on a chair trying to install speakers in a hole in the wall.

"There's something she doesn't want us to know," Sarah said, "and I intend to find out what. We need to learn about Camila." She glanced at Michael.

"I'm the one who should be following up," Michael said.

Sarah opened another box of books and searched.

"What are you looking for?" Michael asked.

"*The Joy of Cooking.*"

Screwdriver in hand, Michael turned to stare.

"I told my book club we'd serve hemlock if the election was disappointing. I'm hoping there's a recipe."

Michael returned to his task. "What are you reading?"

"No one has time to read; we have a designated reader, and it's Marjory this month." She opened another box. *Why Marriages Succeed or Fail* sat fresh and crisp on top, the sales slip protruding from its pages.

"I think families in our states should adopt families in the other states, and give them free subscriptions to the *New York Times,*" Sarah said, "and those in our states could commit to watching a certain amount of Fox News." She emptied the box and began sorting.

Michael lifted a speaker into the cave in the wall.

"I don't get why they think we like the excesses of Hollywood and the music industry any more than they do," Sarah said, standing and walking over to the love seat. Clearing a space, she sat down, and leaned back. Seven stories below, traffic hummed softly on the parkway along the river, and Sarah turned to the window, where green, red, and yellow treetops clashed with the upholstery.

"When I went to the deli this morning," she said, "I saw a young woman reading *Lolita* — Nabokov's *Lolita,* not the one about Tehran — and I was flooded with peace. Some things endure, in spite of elections. Good literature will endure."

"That's because it wasn't on the ballot," Michael said. He stepped down from the chair and put the screwdriver on the shelf. Looking around the apartment, he knocked on the walls, first one, then the other. "Do you feel safe yet?"

"Bloodshed mounts . . ." CNN said.

RACHEL HAD GIVEN Sarah a T-shirt with a picture of Simone de Beauvoir.

Sarah had given Rachel

Word

we were delayed at the grocery store, it
was the all-immigrant night shift at
the 24-hour market, Star, and our
immigrant was Indian, Asian Indian, and he
stopped his cashier duties in the
checkout line to show a small boy ahead
of us some word games and the
boy and his father seemed delighted with

what they were learning, being extra
nice while we waited patiently, shuffling
our paper towels and toilet
paper, well, okay, and a little ice cream, vanilla,
with chocolate sauce, and once the clerk
admired how adroitly the little boy achieved an
answer and the boy said my
friend taught me and I thought that's the most
beautiful

SARAH FINISHED READING Lisa's résumé, and leaned
toward her. "I like the part where you indicate your college degree," she said. They sat at the dining room table,
Sarah ensconced in the head-of-the-table armchair, Lisa
in a side chair. Sarah and Michael had dispensed with
the chandelier in the new dining room, turning the space
into a library, with floor lamps, books, paintings.

"I worry, though," Sarah said, "under current job duties,
if people will get 'Conceptualize non-hierarchical, non-
patriarchal, ethnicity-blind strategies for the exploration of
earth-based solutions to conflict-driven phenomena.'"

"People reading this won't be as uptight as you are,"
Lisa said. "No offense, but I don't think you're qualified
to help with this." She stood. "I *would* like to take you up
on your offer of a ride to Davis Square." Lisa had an ancient VW bug with a daisy on it that spent three-fourths
of the year in the shop.

Random had jumped up when Lisa stood, and was lobbying.

THE NEW-SMELLING elevator carpeting was a splotchy brown, gray, and black so dirt wouldn't show. When pantsuited Mrs. Baker got on at the third floor, and edged closer to the wall as Random investigated her heels, Sarah chatted faster than usual to distract from Lisa's paisley tie over the ~~denim work blouse under the~~ plaid suspenders.

"What's she like?" Lisa asked, when Mrs. Baker got off at the lobby.

"Lovely, keeps to herself."

"If she had a daughter," Lisa said, "who saw you in an elevator and asked her mother what you are like, what would she say?"

Sarah winced. "She'd probably say I was nice, but eccentric, dressing in a sloppy, perhaps bohemian way. In a hurry, wearing baseball caps that say things like — "

"We're here," Lisa said, as the elevator opened noisily at the garage level.

Was Lisa ashamed of her?

By people in general, Sarah wanted to be accepted, approved, included but not invited often.

Oil spots and mysterious streams of water marked the garage floor.

"Tell me about Harvey," Sarah said, in as offhanded

a manner as she could manage, clicking on her seat belt. Lisa was meeting him at the diner.

Turning on the radio, Lisa moved through an irritating array of stations. "He's a great guy, smart, well-read, energetic, hardworking, you'll love him. He knows more about art than you do."

Sarah couldn't suppress hope. Larry had been a petty thief, John was a gambling addict, and Ezekiel had called to tell Lisa he was sleeping with another woman and was that okay. After backing up, Sarah put the car in drive and made another swing at the garage exit. "Is Harvey employed?" she asked in a too-high voice.

"He has a lot of irons in the fire."

The garage doors clanged behind them. "Is he kind?" Sarah asked.

"Kind?"

They pulled onto the street. Redbrick buildings, one as boring as the next.

"You know how spare and simple your writing is?" Lisa said. "I could help you with it."

"Oh, that's nice . . ."

"No, I mean it. I wouldn't mind."

"Thank you. Let's see how things go."

Lisa continued searching for radio stations.

"Public radio is 90.9," Sarah said.

"They have Brits analyzing our political situation."

"Turn it off, then," Sarah said. Left at the post office.

OPEN LATER TO SERVE YOU BETTER. How long would a letter take to reach Latin America?

"Margaret's coming east next month, and we're getting together. Remember Margaret?" Lisa said.

The roommate after Sheila. "She's the one who threw pots, and made that speckled ceramic tea strainer you gave me," Sarah said.

"I remember your birthday but not Mom and Dad's," Lisa said. "When does he come back?"

"Tomorrow."

The Episcopal church at the crossroads was being torn down. Sarah had tried, too, to get Lisa to pick up men at church.

A Greek restaurant next to the woodworking store.

"Do you have any vacation days left?" Sarah asked Lisa.

"Three. Camila asked me to come to Miami, and I'm thinking about it. I like her, but something's not right."

"What?"

"She said you bad-mouthed me."

"I would *never . . .*"

"That's what I mean."

Sarah was rattled by traffic decisions, lanes, cars, lights, horns, and then the silver-roofed diner appeared, and she pulled into the parking lot.

"There's Harvey!" Lisa said.

A sad-eyed youth, cap pulled low over his forehead,

leaned against a Humvee, chunky steel earrings hanging from eyebrows and ears, and baggy, torn, low-slung jeans from his torso.

Lisa lit up, and fastened her eyes on an attractive, well-groomed young man, trimmed hair, lean, wearing what appeared to be a designer suit with his Italian shoes, walking toward her side of the car. Did he know he was gay.

PAPERS SPREAD OUT across the dining room table. A fresh spiral notebook, a dictionary, cue cards with plot points, the last draft, the current draft, Kleenex, a glass of milk, an insurance bill, three tiny ivory figures from China.

Michael came in. "I had a call from Camila."

Sarah pushed her chair back.

"She told me what happened in the park."

She put her pen down.

"She said you told her to stay away from me . . ." Little knives shooting from his eyes. "You've crossed the line."

He intended to slam the door when he stormed out but it petered.

"I'M GOING TO see Magdalena," Michael said, eyeing the bleeding steaks. They were headed toward the bread aisle. "Do you want the cart, or should I take it?"

Crowds swarmed around them; one felt like swooning. Sarah clenched the handle of the empty grocery cart, which had pieces of spinach and plastic embedded in its metal bottom, and steadied herself. She'd tried talking with him; he wasn't having it. It was unlike him not to believe her about Camila. What spell had Camila cast, how did it relate to guilt.

People in the store knew where they were going.

"I'll get milk," Michael said.

"You're supposed to go there last," Sarah said weakly, "so it won't go bad." Her fear and anger bumped up against each other; it took the anger longer to surface.

"Eggs, then," Michael said, before throwing his arms up in the air. "Cereal!" He sprinted down the aisle and she watched him get smaller. She didn't move, tightening her bloodless grip on the cart. Right, left, or straight ahead. Rage frightened her; she felt she could murder.

"Excuse me," a woman with a Spanish accent said, as Sarah dragged her cart to the side so the woman could pass. Sarah gathered herself and bent over to look for oat bread, which could help the heart. When did English muffins explode into so many flavors? He didn't mean it about going to see Magdalena; there would be no turning back.

Michael returned with the kind of raisin bran that has too many raisins, and tossed the box into the cart. "What next?"

Sarah consulted her list. "Paper towels and toilet paper." He always got the wrong kind of each, but he knew where they were located, and it seemed cruel to criticize when he'd been good enough to fetch them. She turned into the next aisle and reached for lentil, sending several soup cans tumbling to the floor, and looked to see who'd been watching as she returned them to the shelf.

Michael reappeared with thin, coarse toilet paper, and thin, coarse, nonabsorbent paper towels, adding beer, honey nuts, and ice cream to the cart. A crash sounded in the aisle behind them, and ahead of them blue-coated employees — their nametags said Aishe and Momalie — continued to position stale food in front of fresh.

Sarah checked the list, but many items were too complicated for Michael. "I'll meet you at the TV dinners." He would get Hungry-Man, she would get the kid dinner with the brownie in it. Arabic music played through the loudspeaker. Sarah needed meat, but didn't want to speak with the butcher in case she said something stupid. She stepped over the red spill on the floor and pushed past the couscous, the pinto beans, and the lo mein to reach the animal crackers denied her as a child.

RANDOM RAN AHEAD of Sarah, pulling on the leash as they neared the door for their walk; several times in their nine-year history he had come close to dislocating her shoulder.

Sarah zipped up her down jacket with one hand, while gripping the red-handled leash with the other. She and Michael had returned to the pet store to get the kind of leash that would be quickly sliced in two by elevator doors slamming shut, after just such a leash saved Random's life the day Sarah stepped off an elevator while he dawdled to investigate a smell in the carpet. Sarah's guilt unending.

It wasn't the first time he had taken a solitary elevator ride since they'd moved to their apartment. He became enthusiastic to the point of hysteria when guests arrived and rushed to meet them when the elevator doors opened, leaping into the elevator to begin the petting and cooing, sometimes staying on when the guest stepped out.

As they exited the building, Sarah hesitated — right or left — the decision usually based on which route would minimize the number of people with whom she'd have to chat.

She chose the right — a few steps and the pleasant, treed territory outside a Harvard office building, with broad windows revealing workers — usually women — in front of computer screens. Sarah liked the corner office with the vintage JFK campaign poster on the wall.

Random performed the first pee in the usual place, under the pine tree, then scurried along a trail outside the redbrick building. He seemed disinclined to pause long enough to poop this early in their walk, and Sarah knew what that meant — several tugs-of-war as she tried to drag him from the trash cans at the entrance to the park. The park was a popular lunch venue, even in cooler weather, and sandwich remains would be tossed at receptacles with varying degrees of accuracy.

Sarah drew him along, continuing to pull on the leash as they passed the benches of people eating; she tried to appear dignified and not as cruel as she must look. Random often coughed loudly at these moments in a choking sort of way, ratcheting up the drama.

From the other direction, a large German shepherd led its owner by the leash; Sarah eyed their progress. When they were a few yards away, Sarah picked Random up and held him until the German shepherd passed, craning its neck to get a better look at Random. Random seemed oblivious to potential dangers. Tail wagging.

He stopped and arched his back in the crouched pooping position, turning his head from side to side so as not to miss anything, the vibrating nose continuing to sniff. He strained. *Please God don't let anyone pass now,* which would distract Random and set them back half an hour.

Sarah had a favorite picture of Michael. In this park. In the pouring rain, Michael's six-foot-two-inch frame bending into the wind to hold an umbrella over Random as Random pooped, torrents of water streaming down Michael's unprotected face.

The time she and Michael clutched each other in the darkened vet's office when he told them the operation had failed and Random was now blind in his right eye.

Sarah had taken him to a dog trainer/psychologist

when he was a puppy, and the man had analyzed him — he had a tiny attention span, was secure and confident, and considered himself Sarah's equal. This last was the area that needed work, the trainer felt, but Sarah was thrilled Random didn't consider himself her superior.

The poop was beginning to emerge. Yes, yes, *yes*. A healthy, solid chunk. Random went bounding off to explore another corner of the universe, and Sarah, too, felt a burden removed, a lightness of being. She picked up after him with a special plastic bag/scooper she'd bought online; you didn't even have to feel the texture of the droppings. She tossed it into a trash can.

Sarah and Michael had adopted him from a litter in Connecticut. They'd walked into a kitchen full of puppies hopping around like Mexican jumping beans, and narrowed the choice to two; Michael felt Random had a more athletic gait than his sister.

Sarah cradled Random in her arms during the two-and-a-half-hour drive back to Boston, stroking and murmuring to him nonstop, trying to salve the trauma of being ripped from the bosom of his family. Random slept the whole way, waking occasionally to lean over and kiss Michael before returning to his slumber.

A couple of weeks later, the woman in Connecticut called to see how he was doing, and Sarah asked, "Could you tell when he was born that he was special?"

Someone had told Sarah and Michael it wasn't good to have your dog sleep with you, so they tried various measures to get Random to sleep other places, and he would pretend to follow their instructions as the night began. Every morning they awoke to find his warm, curled body pressed against their thighs, surely life's sweetest reward.

"Who do you love most?" Sarah and Michael would ask Random. "Run to the person you love most!" As they stood at either end of the hall, a panting Random, ears flying, racing back and forth between them.

Trees and grass and leaves and mounds of dirt — Random barely knew where to start. He ran to circle a tree, seeking the perfect spot to add his mark. The homeless woman's sleeping bag lay lumped under a tree some distance way, although she was nowhere to be seen.

From behind them, a woman and her odd whippet-looking-but-much-larger dog came up and walked alongside them.

"How old is she?" the woman asked, looking at Random.

"He," Sarah said. "He's nine."

"You take good care of him," the woman said, which was perplexing, because what would be the evidence — his breathing?

The woman's dog was brown and tall and slender, almost like a short pony, except for the slender part. Maybe more like a gazelle or a deer. Sarah made some comment to that effect to the woman, who nodded. "My children put antlers on him at Christmas."

Sarah could see it. The sweatered dog stepped gracefully, slowly, biding his time.

Random ignored the new members of their group as he scouted for worthy nuggets in the grass along the pathway. Sarah and Random were on the left side of the walk.

At some point Random must have decided that the right bank offered more potential, and crossed in front of everyone, his blind eye toward them, to get to the other side. When he was halfway across, somehow, in a motion Sarah never noticed but would never forget, the deer-dog moved forward and sank his teeth into Random's head, at the ear. Holding on.

Random shrieked, tried to tear away.

Sarah howled. Deep, bloodcurdling, nonhuman, involuntary screams, the likes of which she'd never heard. Over and over, as she saw in a flash how the event would unfold — Random ripped to pieces — body parts, blood, fur flying. *Something horrible is happening here, something horrible is happening.*

The woman shouted at her large dog, pulled on him.

He refused to release his grip.

Random yelping, Sarah screaming.

It was endless.

Finally the woman succeeded in extricating her dog's teeth from Random.

Sarah picked Random up and ran.

He was quiet.

When they were some distance away, Sarah put him down. She bent over to examine him. Teeth marks on the inside, fleshy part of the ear, no blood immediately apparent;

she couldn't tell about the furry skin around the ear. Random didn't want to keep still for the examination, because, just over that tuft of grass was . . . what? Manure perhaps, some sort of exotic fertilizer . . . He made his zigzag way through the twig-strewn green, peeing here, sniffing there.

Sarah couldn't stop shaking, couldn't, still, think clearly, stunned by the attack, by the otherworldly screams. Should she take Random to the vet immediately? His tail wagging.

They would go back to the apartment where she could observe him.

She nudged Random toward home, and followed him; he knew the way. Sarah walked backward every few steps to make sure the deer-dog wasn't following.

Random trotting ahead, chin high.

Sarah thought about Michael. *Something horrible.*

"HE'S LEAVING THURSDAY to go see Magdalena," Sarah said to Jacob, walking briskly.

He had difficulty keeping up. A police van passed, a man peering through a barred window in the back.

Sarah avoided the tricycle on the right of the sidewalk, the raccoon poop on the left. "I begged him not to," she said, turning back to Jacob. "Then I insisted on going with him." A sycamore shed its bark along the bank of the dimpled river.

Jacob trudged behind.

"He wouldn't listen to me," she called back to him, "saying it was something he had to do alone." She inhaled deeply; the air scraped her throat. She'd told him what could happen if he left. The worst part was not believing her about Camila. *How do you stay married to someone who thinks you're a liar.*

She loathed him.

"Stop it!" Jacob said, grabbing her arm and forcing her to slow down.

"But I'm going as far as Miami with him," she said, "where I'll try to meet with Camila — God knows what she'll do to me — and the aunt, if she'll let me, and catch Michael the second he comes back into the country." He'd better come back soon. She stopped. "Maybe I don't want him back."

She let Jacob take her hand and they continued walking. "Rachel's out of the hospital," she said. "Her brother's going to be here for a few days." She'd asked Rachel why she didn't go home to Idaho when she got sick. *That would be going backward.*

"Let's get something to eat," Jacob said.

"That's all we do."

"We could go to my place," he said.

"I know a restaurant I want to try," she said.

Jacob looked at someone across the street. "He looks familiar."

Sarah followed his gaze. "Yes," she said. "I don't know if he's a type, or a real person."

After people died, Sarah saw them on street corners. The dead people didn't age; they still waved and hopped into their green Triumph convertibles.

"WHY ARE WE HERE?" Jacob asked as they sat on the wooden chairs at the small table, his back to the room; he could see only her.

"Research," Sarah said. "They serve the same food Michael ate and that Magdalena continues to eat, plus some American stuff. Look, the walls are painted the color of the flag." Red, yellow, blue.

"You can't believe this experience will be anything like being there," Jacob said.

"It's the best I can do, for now." She watched him. *Does he ever consider . . .*

The young Latina handed them menus.

"Empanadas." Sarah said. "Those are the meat turn-overs Eric wrote about, and they have fried yucca."

"Sopa de mondongo," she read.

"Tipico paisa," Jacob said. "A typical regional dish, it says — steak, rice, beans, pork strips, eggs, and sweet plantain, I'll have that."

She looked up at him.

"What are you having?" he asked.

"Chicken fajitas."

"I thought that was Mexican."

"I like them."

They gave their order to the waitress. At the next table, an Anglo teenage boy with a Latin man. *How would Jacob's son feel about me?*

At the furthest table, six attractive Latin men and women, stylish, sophisticated, one of them black. A muted television near the ceiling rolled out images from a Spanish-language movie titled *Cult of the Dead;* a man with a gun crept through a house. During breaks there were ads for AT&T, Wendy's, and a television series titled

"Look," Sarah said, pointing to a heavy couple on a colorful print hanging on the wall. "That's the painter who's so popular there, what's his name, with the oversized figures, you know, Pablo Escobar collected him."

"Botero," Jacob said.

She looked at the fat figures. "He doesn't like people, does he?"

"Where's your cross?" Jacob asked.

Sarah put a hand to her throat. "I'm afraid if I wear it people will think I'm an extremist. I have renewed sympathy for moderate Muslims."

"Take me to church. If it's important to you, it's important to me."

"I can't decide which one, I have trouble with intermediaries."

A tray of dishes clattered to the floor.

"She's not omnipotent," Sarah said, eyeing the broken plates. "God."

A John le Carré paperback stuck out of Jacob's pocket. "He's a good writer," Sarah said, pointing to the book.

"Literary and popular," Jacob said. "It's possible."

"Rare."

"How's Random?"

"When I take him to the park, now that it's colder, the homeless woman and I are frequently the only ones there unless it's lunchtime, and it feels awkward not talking with her. I know if I say hello it would be all over, I'd have to take care of her for the rest of her life, I'm no good at in-between. Michael's opposed to our taking care of her for the rest of her life."

"Middle-class people want sympathy because they have to look at poor people," Jacob said.

Sarah didn't have the coloring to blush, but this is what it would feel like.

On television the women were terrified.

"Tell me again why you're not perfect," she said.

"I don't like to cuddle in bed, I don't like different types of food to touch on my plate, and when I'm at home I have to eat with a special spoon I had as a child. I'm addicted to expensive shoes."

The waitress brought their food, and Sarah stabbed a chicken strip with her fork and swished it into her rice. "How was your lecture?" she asked beneath the flickering *Cult of the Dead*.

"You don't have to go to Miami," Jacob said. "You could move in with me."

PART THREE

People rushed to and from all directions while Sarah and Michael studied each other at a crowded intersection at Miami International Airport. It could have been Brazil, Argentina, Venezuela.

He shifted his suitcase from one hand to the other. He had dandruff on his shoulder, but she didn't brush it off this time. Let Magdalena see it.

SARAH SAT ON an ocean-facing bench near Camila's apartment building, with two days to kill before she visited with Amelia, Camila's aunt, on Thursday; Camila said she'd meet with Sarah on Friday. Restaurants and discos pressed on either side of Camila's white art deco building, and a woman wearing a thong bathing suit skated down the street. It would be hard to pay for a place in this building unless Camila had supplementary sources of income.

Liberated or escaped parrots perched on window ledges, trees. A man and woman clutching a real estate guide and pushing a wheelbarrow full of money raced down the street toward a nest of condominiums. That part Sarah made up.

Does the sun reflect more brilliantly from sun and water, or from snow? Using her hand as a visor, she peered up through the haze of a spiked palm to the fiery orb melting into blue. On the beach, colorful umbrellas perched along the shore as if primping, doing their nails; the ocean was still, waiting. A woman wearing a head scarf carried a sack of books.

SARAH LAY BACK on the motel's pink and green flowered bedspread, thick and rough as tarp, phone cradled under her chin, listening to Michael explain that he couldn't come back on the day he'd said. Why was he twisting this knife? A seascape hung on the far wall, the frothy tips of the waves iridescent. What looked small could become a tsunami.

Sarah's side of the bed was turned down; the other was locked shut.

"Magdalena killed Eric," Michael said, his voice breaking.

On the television, smoke poured out of an exploding jeep in a desert.

"PLEASE EXCUSE THINGS," Amelia said, opening the door for Sarah and gesturing at the apartment.

Short and thick with prominent moles, Camila's aunt had dyed red hair piled on top of her head, with strays. Sarah hoped Magdalena looked like that.

Camila had declined Sarah's invitation to join her.

Sarah entered the apartment, and Amelia, wearing what looked like a muumuu, picked up newspapers from the floor and a jacket from the back of a chair and carried them to a table in the dining room. She pointed to the sofa, and Sarah took a seat in front of a large ashtray overflowing with lipstick-stained cigarette butts. A glass of something with melting ice waited on an end table, and sofa pillows littered the floor. On a shelf, a leather-bound set of Cervantes.

Sarah's own poor housekeeping couldn't be blamed on her mother, as her mother was likely to return a magazine to the magazine rack while you were reading it.

Amelia had taken a seat and crossed the plump legs terminating in flip-flops. Now that Sarah and Michael knew Magdalena was responsible for Eric's death, Amelia was no longer reluctant to talk.

"The night Magdalena and Eric departed the guerrilla camp to save our Poppa, it was raining. She told me Eric was *muy triste* to leave his friends, but he would do anything for Magdalena, and Magdalena must save her Poppa.

"Magdalena said Eric told her not to take anything,

not even the small wooden horse he'd carved, it would awaken suspicion.

"She left out of the camp first, then Eric. She waited for him at a place they arranged." Amelia looked at Sarah. "Magdalena told it with care. You will hear every word.

"They walked in the rain, but didn't mind the rain, I think, because, you see, they'd grown used to it. They'd become strong soldiers, such a long time fighting in the mountains."

Amelia took a sip of black coffee. "Magdalena was a big girl, from young. Tall, without fear. I was the older one, you see, I was my mother's girl. I remember our mother, Magdalena does not.

"Magdalena ran wild, she was Poppa's girl.

"He loved to see her ride, and they took long trips into the countryside, and he spoke with her about animals and plants, and sometimes she stayed overnight in the campo, even when she was young. Poppa would take her hunting with the men, so proud, she was the only girl.

"He taught her to use a gun, and she could shoot a living animal and not blink." Amelia emitted a hollow laugh. "I would cry to see the eye of the fish we ate.

"Once Magdalena shot a wild boar."

Amelia lit a cigarette. "Particularly after our mother died, Poppa was important to her. Sometimes she rode without a blanket or saddle, and once stood barefoot on the back of a horse as it ran. She chose the difficult ones. She looked to see if Poppa was watching — she made him laugh. I was helping in the kitchen, there were things to be done.

"When Magdalena went to university, she changed, and our father didn't laugh. She painted slogans on buildings and marched — that's what it was to be a student. Some of it was for fun — they were children, playing, Magdalena liked the notice.

"She sent Poppa books; she wanted him to learn what she saw, but he slammed the books to the floor. I was helping at home, I was in university Rodriga."

She looked at her cigarette. "But that's not what you came to learn.

"When our father was imprisoned, he was kept in a tent on a hillside, a three-day walk from where he was captured, he told us.

"There would be a guard outside the tent, but sometimes the guard would be asleep, or drunk. They were children.

"Behind a banyan tree, Magdalena and Eric waited and spied on my father's tent, and it was cold. It gets cold in the mountains stabbing you inside. She told me all of this.

"The guard seemed to sleep at the end, and they moved, and when they walked past the guard, Magdalena saw a rosary out of his pocket, although communists do not have God.

"Eric and Magdalena moved to the back of the tent, and Eric sliced a cut with a machete, and they crawled through, where my father was tied to a post.

"My father was not wholly surprised to see them, he had hoped for this, but he was quiet, he knew they were in high danger.

"Eric and Magdalena cut his ropes, and the three climbed out the hole in the tent."

Amelia leaned forward. "I should tell you Camila and I were already living in Miami at this time, as I came here after Rodrigo died."

She hesitated. "Our father thought it was the safe thing, as Rodrigo had joined the group of men who were trying to protect the ranchers from the guerrilleros. Oh, but that was not how he died, eh? It was in a mudslide, from the earthquake."

She cocked her head at Sarah, who nodded.

"Magdalena sent Camila to me when she was three years old. We were in wonder that the guerrilleros let Camila stay so long.

"Magdalena and Eric and our Poppa began running away from the camp where he'd been tied, but with care, so as not to wake anyone. It was not as fast as it could be, and the jungle so full, sometimes you have to cut your own path. It was late at night, eh? Dark, yes? And they had to walk across a muy horrible swinging bridge, made of vines, both the bottom and the railing, over a deep valley, and the rain didn't stop.

"Magdalena told she had been much afraid that day and had not been able to eat, but chewed some coca leaves like the Indians, and the day before, there had been only a little rice, and a piece of sardine from a can.

"The guard must have woken and Magdalena and Eric heard shouts and then the sounds of people following. Magdalena and Eric and my father ran fast, but the noise came closer.

" 'You and your father go ahead,' Eric said. 'I'll draw them away and catch up at the river.'

"Now this made Magdalena mad — he had promised in advance they would not separate, as this, above all, she did not want. She argued with Eric, but he had made his mind, although she fought more, he overruled, as he did.

"Magdalena and our father left him. Magdalena said she shuddered so much she grabbed one hand with the other and tried to make it still, but it wouldn't. They ran faster — sometimes running downhill is more unsteady than uphill — and they fell, and had to pick up. Remember, the night was white with fog, eh? Slippery, wet mud, full of mist; mist leaves in the morning.

"After a while of running, they heard nothing. 'Let's rest here,' Magdalena said, when they were at two large boulders with bamboo growing on top and alongside. She gave my father an antibiotic capsule, and tried to bandage his arm, but could not stop her shaking. My father did what she said, he was weak, a small boy.

"They stayed for a long time, but heard nothing but the

running river. Magdalena has such strong feeling, from her head to her feet, and she grew in anger at Eric. She looked over at her frail Poppa, leaning against stone.

"Suddenly the mountain was shrieking, with gun-shots, and crashing branches. Magdalena knelt in posi-tion with her gun, behind the boulder. There were more shouts and then the sound of someone so close she could hear panting, and as the clouds rolled past the moon, she saw, raised in the air, a hand gripping a machine gun. She fired."

Amelia turned to Sarah, who looked at Amelia's feet.

Amelia put out the cigarette she hadn't smoked. Be-hind her, a chipped gold-leaf plate, a replica of an Inca plate from the Gold Museum, sat on a wooden table by the balcony.

"It was many years before Magdalena told it," Amelia said. "I am sorry for her, but she should not have joined with such people." She rose and went to the kitchen, where a refrigerator door opened and ice rattled.

Sarah faced the window, where there was no ocean.

Amelia returned with the glass and reclaimed her seat. No one spoke.

"I'd like to know about Camila," Sarah said.

Amelia waved her arms, as if shooing a fly.

It seemed Camila had been a bed wetter. Then she'd had trouble learning to read. Mostly she was silent. The scholarship to college had been a shock. It had been ex-pensive, caring for her; Amelia's salary as a bookkeeper could barely cover the rent. When she was in third grade, Camila had given half her lunch every day to that shabby Rosita from down the street — the lunch Amelia had made. Sometimes she gave her clothes, too, when they still fit. So often Camila had been sick and had to be taken to the doctor. She was never well, that girl. When she was a teenager, the men called at all hours; she stayed out late at night, Amelia couldn't sleep, and didn't know the men's parents. There was the time Camila left the window open during the storm, all of the furniture ruined.

SARAH HAD PUSHED the details of Eric's death, everything, into an out-of-reach pocket, since she could.

The motel elevator was occupied by a young man holding *Dwell* magazine; the metallic doors slammed shut and the cab descended. Decorating a house could be fun.

The buzz-cropped young man pulled dark glasses out of his flowered shirt pocket and put them on.

You can buy the perfect object, say an exquisite chair, and put it in a room with other things and all of a sudden the room looks dreadful, because it doesn't work as a whole, although the chair is a work of art.

The man looked at his flip-flops.

The elevator doors opened and he pushed past Sarah to exit.

Sarah followed him into the goldfish-carpeted lobby. *Or paintings, the most beautiful or interesting painting in*

the world can make a room look busy if there is one other
object in the room, which is why paintings that are fat, sin-
gle-color blobs are the easiest to decorate with, and why it's
so hard to use oriental rugs.

The man veered off to the door to the street and Sarah headed for the café, where a few patrons sat at booths separated by ferns and palms on an uneven brick floor. She perched at the counter and ordered Caesar salad, trying to see the ocean through the window, but a white stretch limo, surrounded by pedestrians peering inside, blocked her view.

The silver counter stool was slippery, and Sarah tried to find a comfortable, stable position. The café's tan walls looked like cork. She foraged in her purse and removed a bottle of Tums, pouring three into the palm of her hand, as a woman sitting next to her watched. *I could be tak-* *ing these for calcium.* Last week she'd used a dermatitis prescription labeled "The exact mechanism of action is not known."

She held the Tums. Camila, Camila.

THE DOOR OF THE J-Lo Rode Me taxi slammed behind her, as Sarah got out near Camila's building. Bathing-suit stores crowded around Versace, and foot traffic on the sidewalks was dense, theatrical; Sarah remembered when South Beach had been pocked with warehouses.

More parrots.

Two policemen sat in an unmarked car.

She was fifteen minutes early; the driver had been re-
sourceful. Jacob had told her it was a mistake to go to
Camila's apartment alone; she should pick neutral territory, with witnesses.

A few steps led to the glass doors of the stucco apartment building, which opened onto turquoise carpet,
where two frail, white-haired women snoozed on wooden
chairs in a corner of the lobby. The odor of mold. Sarah
pressed the elevator button and double-checked Camila's
apartment number. A slim young man with a lavender-
collared German shepherd stepped out as Sarah entered
the mirrored elevator.

She got out on the ninth floor and knocked on Camila's
door, which popped open at her touch, loud Latin music
emanating from the apartment. A newspaper lay on the
floor, and Sarah picked it up, waiting, but when Camila
didn't appear, she knocked again, trying not to widen the
gap between the door and the wall.

"Camila? . . . Camila!"

Had she forgotten she'd invited her. Did she know
Michael had gone to see Magdalena.

She must have left the door open so Sarah would come
in. Was that wise? Sarah gave the door a tap, entered, and
closed the door behind her. How could she stand the music that loud?

Brightly colored Tibetan rugs sat on white carpet, and
tables were Plexiglas, the sofa leather. The coffee table

held a half-eaten sandwich and an empty Coke bottle, and clothes hung on the back and arms of the couch. A wet towel scrunched on the floor, alongside several pairs of shoes. Sarah listened for the sound of a shower, but heard nothing over the music. She supposed Camila could be setting a trap.

A balcony opened off the living room, and Sarah craned her neck for a view of the ocean but the balcony, with a hibiscus bush pressed against black grillwork, faced the parking lot. Pale blue chairs huddled around a glass table in the dining room, and papers sat on the top of a bird-of-paradise place mat — a note?

Closer inspection revealed the pile to be bills and junk mail, and Camila's open purse sat nearby, where a set of keys had been tossed. Sarah looked up into the canary yellow kitchen, and caught the bend of Camila's elbow — she was sitting at the kitchen table.

"Camila!"

She didn't hear.

Sarah entered the room, where Camila's body lay slumped over the kitchen table next to a line of white powder.

"ANOTHER FIVE MINUTES and it would have been too late," Sarah said into the phone to Jacob, pacing on her tiny motel balcony. "She was having convulsions; they said her respiratory system would have failed within

moments. That's the way with cocaine, the doctor said."
Sarah had called 911.

Breathing heavily for both of them, she sat down. "You
can OD from snorting." She scratched the soles of her
feet on the golf-green carpet as she sank into the collaps-
ible folding chair, parts of her anatomy drooping through
slats. "They're keeping her in the hospital for observation,
then her aunt will take her to her apartment for a couple of days." She stood and paced again. "Should I tell
Michael?"

"Not when he's out of the country and can't do anything about it." Was this good advice, or did Jacob have
an ulterior motive.

Sarah leaned over the railing and twisted to the left,
trying for a view of ocean.

THE MOTEL BED sank in the middle, she couldn't move.
The blinds were drawn, light was skewed, and it was either early morning or late afternoon, time for breakfast
or time for dinner, late for something. Torpor permeated
every crevice of the room and sat heavily on her chest, as
she ached for sleep.

CAMILA SLEPT AS Sarah sat in the wooden chair at the
foot of the hospital bed. The amaryllis Sarah had sent
stood on the bedside table, next to the assortment from

Camila's office and a crystal vase of long-stemmed red roses without a card.

A crucifix hung above the bed. You didn't dare complain.

The sun shines here no matter what. Falling on Spanish-language magazines and *Newsweek.*

They moved from one hermetically sealed air-conditioned unit to the next; outdoor sounds were also prohibited. Her glasses fogged when she left a building.

"Did she want you to find her dead?" Rachel had asked.

Did she want me to save her. Could I.

Rachel had fallen in love with her home health care worker and was planning her future, her studies, her career. Sometimes Delores became frightened at Rachel's symptoms and called the doctor in a panic, but Rachel wasn't moving.

Random had thrown up, but was okay now, Lisa had said.

A middle-aged man with thinning hair appeared at Camila's doorway, working a Dolphins baseball cap around in his fingers like a rosary, wedding ring glinting.

FROM THE BALCONY to the framed exit instructions, Sarah walked the length of the motel room, and returned.

"I *can't* come back now," Michael said on the phone. "I'll

be back in three days, I know I said that before, but this time for sure. I'll explain when I get there, it's complicated."

Sarah stopped. "I am telling you, with all the clarity and emphasis I can muster, you *must* come back now. If you value your marriage at all, it's essential that you come back. *Now.* I cannot stress this enough."

"I'm sorry," Michael said.

BENDING TO ACCOMMODATE the low showerhead, as lukewarm water dribbled rivulets across her shivering limbs, Sarah rubbed the small, thin bar of soap over her thigh, her calf. She rinsed, turned off the water, and stepped out of the rusted tub onto the thin, pink bath mat, and tried to dry with a towel the size of a dishcloth. Water dripping from the showerhead thumped into the tub like cannonballs.

PRESSING THE PHONE to her ear, she listened to it ring at Amelia's apartment, ringing, ringing.

SHE SAT IN AN aisle seat on the plane, holding her book, *Florida.* They were out of peanuts.

Someone had left a newspaper. "Terrorist Chatter Down."

At Boston's Logan Airport, she headed toward baggage pickup; they were out of carts.

After waiting in line for an hour, she got a taxi, and gave the address. It was midnight.

SHE LAY BACK on the cool, pale sheet, hair tumbled, and drew him to her.

She gasped, and closed her eyes.

SITTING ON THE BED, she tucked her bare toes and legs under Jacob's shirt, and sipped cranberry juice, as morning light illuminated the drawing of a dreaming woman on his bedroom wall. He lay on the bed, sheet pulled to his waist.

Too soon to absorb the significance of what they'd done.

In a corner of the room, an abstract mahogany sculpture, and on the far wall, a black and white Kathe Kollwitz print. "When Michael thinks about death," Sarah said, "he worries he won't be able to climb all the mountains, fish all the streams, raft the Grand Canyon."

"Did you reach Camila?" Jacob asked.

She nodded.

"And?'

"Better." She leaned back against him. "I need you to talk."

"Why do you talk so much?" he asked.

"For the same reason Michael won't; to keep this from happening." She covered her eyes.

LATER.

"According to Kay Redfield Jamison," Jacob said, "a girl's boarding school had to be shut down for a number of years because of an epidemic of uncontrollable laughter that began with three cases and spread to hundreds."

Sarah smiled.

Jacob got out of bed, faced her. "The category is art." The broad shoulders above the narrow-hipped, rainbow-colored briefs

"Charades? Sarah asked.

"Simpler." He imitated someone painting at an easel, then took an imaginary whack at his left ear, before doubling over, as if in pain, clutching the left side of his head.

"Van Gogh," Sarah said. "Although I don't know which ear it was."

"Me neither, your turn."

Sarah sprang out of bed, thought for a second, then began executing poorly remembered, arm-fluttering ballet leaps across the hardwood floor.

"Degas," he said.

She sat, he stood. "Movies." He put his fists to his eyes and rotated them, frowning and moaning.

"*The Crying Game*," she said.

Sarah stood, and moved her hands in a wave from the top of her head to her shoulders in an attempt to indicate a pageboy, then sat on a chair, picked up an imaginary pen, looked to the air for inspiration, and began to write on an imaginary tablet. Suddenly she gasped and rose to her feet, as if she'd seen something in the distance, then fell to her knees, and pressed the palms of her hands to her heart, looking with adoration at the object of her gaze.

Jacob was silent, and she held her hands out to him in question, but he shook his head.

"*Shakespeare in Love*," she said.

"The category is politicians," he said, standing and contorting his pressed-together lips in a twisted, lopsided position, adopting a deer-caught-in-the-headlights expression.

"Too easy," Sarah said and moved to the center of the room. "The category is terrorists."

"Sarah."

"Okay. Cartoon characters." She glanced at her watch.

"What are you doing for Rachel?" he asked.

"Bearing witness."

SARAH LAY LENGTHWISE on the foot of the flowered, duvet-covered bed, while Rachel was tucked right side up, under the sheets, describing her first day of school, rushing home to teach her younger brother what she'd learned, so nothing would separate them. Rachel looked more beautiful than ever, the high cheekbones prominent on the emaciated face, her pink nightgown like a necklace between chin and sheet.

They were quiet, remembering six.

"Bobby Patson," Sarah said. "I was the only girl he invited to his birthday party. We played trucks." Bobby's hair slicked back in a manner she later found odious.

"How were you at dodgeball?" Rachel asked.

"World-class." The sweet smell of rubber.

"I decorated my valentine shoe box with lace doilies and heart candy," Rachel said.

"I received twenty-two valentines," Sarah said. "One from Tommy Jervin, two from secret admirers."

"I got to clean the blackboard and erasers after class," Rachel said.

"Got to?"

"And then I was allowed to arrange the books by height on the little shelf in the back of the room."

"When it rained, we played wild animals and hid in our caves under the desks during recess," Sarah said. "You had to growl in character."

Rachel turned to the white-shuttered windows.

"Shall I open them?" Sarah asked.

Rachel shifted until she faced the other direction.

A book titled *How to Make Meetings Work* and a volume of poetry sat on the bedside table next to three rows of pills, and Sarah stood and opened the poetry book to where it was marked; Rachel had thirty-four pages to go.

"What's your middle name?" Sarah asked.

"Anne. Why?"

"I realized I didn't know."

"Why did Michael ask you to meet him in Washington?" Rachel asked.

"To join him and Magdalena. The ex-guerrilla has become a businesswoman; Michael's going to introduce her to someone he knows at a bank there, a possible investor."

Rachel rubbed her thumb across the hem of the sheet.

Sarah sat on the bed. "We've had long phone conversations. He sounds . . ." She lay back. "I'm going down a day early; there's something I want to do." She inhaled. "Then Magdalena's going to Miami to see Camila, since Camila has agreed to let her visit."

"Why did Michael stay with Magdalena all week?"

Sarah hoped Rachel meant it when she said she wanted to talk of other things. "They had to locate Eric's body, and bury him. Apparently he'd been tossed into some sort of pauper's grave."

"What about his sister."

"They called her, and after she spoke with Michael and Magdalena, she agreed that Eric would want to stay in Latin America." *We buried him under a ceiba tree on land that used to belong to Magdalena's father,* Michael had said. *Red and yellow orchids climb the riverbank, you can hear the rush of water. At certain times of day, the shadow of the mountain finds him.*

Sarah sank into the comforter. *The shadow of the mountain* . . .

"Now," Rachel said.

Sarah handed her the crutches and helped Rachel-with-her-pouch into the brightly lit, mirrored, undenying bathroom, grabbing a pair of rubber gloves along the way.

"Call Susan," Rachel said. "Tell her to reschedule my presentation for next week."

Where will you be, when I'm like this?

THEY SAT ON a bench in Lafayette Park, across Pennsylvania Avenue from the barricaded White House, Michael in the middle, Magdalena on his left, Sarah on his right. Sarah bent over to hear what Magdalena was saying.

Magdalena's chin-length dark hair ran smooth and sleek; silver earrings arched toward her black leather jacket. The blue eyes. Her face only mildly weathered, enough to be interesting. Long red nails pushed hair behind her ears; the perfume was pale, clean. She was slim and looked nothing like her sister.

It no longer mattered.

Sarah and Magdalena wore identical black scarves.

A few pedestrians walked the pathways through the park, where brittle, brown leaves lay scattered on grass beneath empty branches, and a bearded, legless man in khaki fatigues leaned against a tree and held a cardboard sign: IRAQ WAR VETERAN.

Magdalena spoke slowly, in low, husky Spanish. She wore a Minnie Mouse watch.

Michael turned to Sarah. "It was a terrible meeting."

"What happened?"

"Gus was a jerk. The terms of the loan were outrageous — it would have destroyed her company."

"I'm sorry," Sarah said, looking at Magdalena. At lunch, before she and Michael met with the banker, Magdalena had explained to Sarah what her business was, but Sarah had forgotten, and now it would be embarrassing to ask. Something about computers, possibly related to the newspaper business.

"Gracias for kindness for Camila," Magdalena said to Sarah.

Michael bounced his leg; the bench shook.

Magdalena winked at Sarah. Magdalena had been trying to stop smoking, and pulled out the battered roll of LifeSavers she'd shared at lunch, unwrapping until she reached cherry, Sarah's favorite. Sarah accepted.

Two Saudi men wearing traditional garb walked toward Pennsylvania Avenue.

"You were going to tell me," Sarah said to Magdalena. "About what happened when you went home, after you left the guerrillas."

Magdalena glanced at Michael, who gave her a tight smile before turning to Sarah. He looked back at Magdalena, who crossed the long legs, gazing across the street at the gated White House. She spoke in Spanish.

"Could she speak in English?" Sarah asked. Throughout lunch, Sarah had struggled with Magdalena's Spanish and Michael's translation, as Magdalena must have struggled with her English, and Sarah was suffering from language fatigue.

Michael spoke to Magdalena in Spanish.

She responded in Spanish.

"She says, if you don't mind, she's more comfortable speaking in Spanish, about a thing so difficult."

"*Mi Papá se fue ~~~~ y ~~~~ la ciudad,*" Magdalena said. "*Mi Papá volvió a su hacienda aunque era peligroso. No pude convencerlo de que no lo hiciera. No me escuchaba. Mi Papá era un hombre muy decidido.*"

"After I left the guerrilleros, I returned to the capital," Michael translated. "My father returned to his ranch, although it was dangerous, I couldn't stop him, he wouldn't listen."

"*Al principio, me quedé con amigos, los que todavía tenía de la universidad. Yo trataba de vivir escondida por no sentirme segura saliendo de la casa. Pasaba todo el tiempo leyendo. Mi Papá me mandaba dinero.*"

"At first I stayed with friends, I still had friends from the university, and I tried to live quietly, barely feeling safe to leave the house. I was all the time reading. My Poppa sent money."

"*Después de muchos meses sin nada de problemas o atentados de ellos yo tenía mucho más confianza. Salía de la casa con más frequencia y finalmente solicité un puesto*"

como secretaria para un diario. Obtuve el puesto y even-
tualmente tomé mi propio apartamento. También yo me
comunicaba con otra guerrillera, una compañera, que tam-
bién se fue de ellos."

"Months passed without a thing happening, and I became more brave and began to depart from the house. I
applied to have a job, it was to be a secretary at a newspaper, and I received the job, and was able to move into
my own apartment. I had communication with one other
guerrilla, who had also deserted."

Magdalena interrupted Michael. *"Había rosas en el patio*
detrás del edificio y el dueño me permitía cada día quitar
algunas de las frescas de colores rojo, rosado y amarillo."

He nodded. "There were rosebushes in the courtyard
in the back of the building, and the owner let her cut
flowers every day, red, pink, yellow."

"Durante dos años viví así. Tomé clases por la noche
en la universidad y luego me sentía normal de nuevo.
Imagínate cómo era salir de noche. También augmentaron
mis responsabilidades en el diaro y me dieron un puesto más
administrativo. Yo tenía nuevos amigos."

"For two years, I lived this way. I took classes at the
university at night, and began to feel normal. To go out
at night, you can imagine. I was handed a promotion to
an administrative function, and had new amigos."

"Pero un día alguien golpéo a la puerta."

"One day a knock came to the door."

Magdalena stood and walked over to a creased, empty

brown paper bag on the grass, bent to pick it up, and placed it in a trash can before returning to the bench.

"Durante años yo tenía miedo de que los guerrilleros o sus compañeros me buscaran. Pero los que me encontraron fueron los paramilitares uniformados. Y recordé las historias y tenía mucho miedo."

"For years I dreamt that the guerrilleros or their friends would find me, but it was paramilitaries, wearing fatigues, who came for me. I had heard the many stories; my fear was great."

Sarah stopped hearing the Spanish.

"They knew about my past activities — witnesses told about my life with the guerrilleros, some things they get from torture.

"I'm not sure from where the orders came, or they acted on their own. They offered a pact with El Diablo, saying if I would show where some guerrilla camps were, they would save me, and they made dark threats on Camila, they would find her in Miami. They told me this."

Sarah felt nauseated and moved closer to Michael, who took her hand.

"I would not agree except for Camila."

Sarah let go of Michael's hand, and walked around to Magdalena's side of the bench, sitting next to her, patting her knee stupidly. Magdalena continued to look straight ahead, acknowledging Sarah with a small nod. Sarah had read about survivors who recited their stories like robots.

"I thought I could take them to old camps no longer used, thinking, if I am careful, I can avoid any meeting with the guerrillas, as I knew not only their trails, but also their habits, and signals. If I picked up on signs they were near, my intention was to lead my captors in another way.

"The men drove me into the mountains by truck, over rough roads, and we traveled for two days, stopping the first night in a small town of campesinos with a pink stucco church with a broken steeple. I had told the broad area of the first camp where Eric and I had been, which was in foothills, and I didn't think it was used in the present. Eric called it Camp Feet Wet, because of the rain, you see, he had always the name for things. He called me Fuego, and Camila he named Chispa, like little fire."

She was embarrassed by her revelations.

"The dirt road came to its end, and we had to depart from the truck, and began hiking one of the trails, very tall.

"Sweltering sun changed places with hitting rain, and mud was to the ankle. One man was stung by a scorpion, and we passed a banana grove, sugarcane, large-billed toucans. The machetes were much in use. It was slow, and the men were frustrated, in particular when, by the end of day, they'd found not a piece of guerrillas or guerrilla camp. They were muy determinado.

"We came near a small village; most who lived there were Indian. Young boys squatted in a half circle beside a mango tree, staring at the soldiers, and the soldiers asked for information about guerrilleros, but the villagers said they knew nothing.

"The men were hungry and cold, and made the decision to spend the night, a night filled with lightning.

"They rose the next morning irritable from uncomfortable sleeping arrangements and a lack of good prospects, one man opening his eye to a tarantula when he woke.

"They became sure that the villagers were in favor of the guerrilleros, or perhaps even rebels themselves. They needed to be shown a lesson."

Magdalena rose and walked over to pick up an ice cream wrapper on the sidewalk, which she deposited in a trash can before returning to her place on the bench.

"The men marched out across the village. By now the anger was boiling. They had forgotten me, I stood within the doorway to one of the huts."

Magdalena was silent.

"Okay?" Michael asked.

After the American Civil War, post-traumatic stress disorder was referred to as "soldier's heart."

How was this story reminding Michael of Vietnam.

"The soldiers went to each house, kicking at doors, shooting who lived there."

The bones in Sarah's spine contracted.

"At some times they threw grenades into homes of branches and leaves, which exploded into fire. One grenade failed, but they had another.

"Villagers walking the paths were machine-gunned,

their bodies dancing before they fell to the mud, and children and old women cried and ran to their families — they were shot as well, not a person did they leave."

Magdalena was breathing funny. Sarah and Michael simultaneously put their arms around her, meeting in the middle.

"Huts and fields were set to fire, pigs and chickens sliced open. Squealing hogs, squawking chickens. Still today I hear the crack of fire."

Michael seemed to shake, although he'd heard the story before.

Twenty Chinese men carrying briefcases walked toward the White House.

"It was nothing but confusion, and I ran to the woods, shrinking behind a tree next to a coca bush, my eyes burning from smoke, and I watched to see which direction the soldiers would flee.

"But they didn't flee, not immediately. Shooting was not the end. They began chopping — heads, ears, breasts . . ."

Magdalena put a hand to her stomach, and narrowed her eyes. "The village was wet with blood.

"Black, matted hair.

"Something from hell was coming in a near hut — cries, and pleas for mercy."

Her voice was scratchy. "On a dirt path, a young girl gasped and dropped to the ground. The age of my cousin. She crawled in her blood a few feet, stopping when one of the paramilitaries walked close. It was so quiet of a sudden, like under the water. But then the soldier saw, and came for her."

A vein at her temple pulsed.

Sarah pulled her jacket tight against the wind.

"Her straw shoe had come off when she fell. It lay upon the mud.

"A small shoe."

Magdalena was motionless.

Michael, too.

Sarah strengthened her grip on Magdalena's shoulder. The wind picked up.

"Magdalena got . . . back to the city." Michael was barely audible. He looked across the barricaded street. "All sides . . . atrocities."

Sarah couldn't hear him.

He eyed an approaching vehicle. The limousine neared the gatehouse.

It was freezing.

MICHAEL HELD SARAH'S hand as they walked toward his rental car. Government workers began streaming through the park on their way home, their boxy suits more conservative than those in New York or on Boston's Newbury Street. In a corner of the park, people and placards gathered for the next protest.

She would have trouble keeping Magdalena's tale in a pocket.

"Do you think she'll make her plane?" Sarah asked.

He looked at his watch, nodded. "She should be in Miami in a couple of hours." He studied Sarah. "I thought you'd be nervous about meeting her."

They walked past the Hay-Adams.

"Yesterday," Sarah said, "I spent the day in the city. I walked all over; I went to every office I'd ever worked in. Monuments, museums, government buildings. I drove across Memorial Bridge, past the Pentagon.

"I saw the heightened security, the F-16s, the anti-aircraft guns, the police cars, the helicopters, the surface-to-air missiles, the concrete barriers. In front of some of the museums, they've put huge pots of flowers on top of the barricades, as if we wouldn't notice they're barricades."

They passed the old Russian embassy. "I realize how foolish it is. To think we can be safe."

They crossed the street and turned. On a TV in a store window, a white-gloved Marine in dress blues leaned over to hand a folded American flag to a seated woman with bent head.

A slow-moving, smoke-spouting bus.

"Bill's going to buy my motorcycle," Michael said.

Sarah tried to appear neutral. A China Shipping truck rushed into town.

"I called Camila," Michael said. "She's coming for Christmas, thanks for suggesting that.

"I've spoken with some drug counselors," he added.

"It's going to take more than that," Sarah said. "A lot more."

He nodded. "More than that. I know what you're thinking," he said. "You're thinking maybe Eric was Camila's dad."

Not breathing.

"On the plane to D.C.," he said, "Magdalena mumbled something about how much safer it was for Camila to have a father who wasn't a guerrilla. And there would have been the stigma."

"So."

"I think . . ." He took a few steps. "I'm going to leave it up to them, Camila and Magdalena. I feel like I owe . . . him."

He threw an arm in front of Sarah to keep her from stepping into the path of an oncoming car.

"I wish you'd come with me when I go to London next time," he said, the Washington Monument visible behind him.

"I thought you didn't want me on your trips," Sarah said, "that I'd get in the way, the frantic pace of the meetings."

"I thought you didn't want to go," he said.

She shook her head. "We could take the tube to that interesting restaurant near King's Cross."

They walked. "How's Rachel?" Michael asked.

"I've spent most of the last year thinking she was deep in denial," Sarah said. "It has only recently occurred to me that what I thought was denial might actually be bravery." She kicked at nothing. "We're throwing her a birthday party."

"You can do that in a hospice? I thought hospice was about resignation."

"Acceptance. If Camila's coming for Christmas, she could come early and go to the party, everyone will be there." Rachel had insisted that family and friends visit in early morning; she'd done her research, and knew that was when most people die.

"Is your friend Jacob coming to the party?"

Sarah paused. She put her arm through his. "Jacob was a fantasy. He doesn't exist."

Michael froze.

"Think about it," she said. "How many heterosexual men do you know who are sensitive, supportive, witty, terrific cooks, lovers of great art and literature, who will listen to me, or any woman, endlessly?"

He thought about it.

It was persuasive.

"What about the times you met him for coffee or ran into him?" he asked.

"Made up."

"Why?" He winced, and held up his hand to stop her from answering.

She squeezed his arm. "If it helps, you could think of him as an angel."

It didn't.

They continued walking, Sarah glancing up at him from time to time to gauge his expression, the grooved brow.

"Let's drive by our old place," he said.

THE CAR SLOWED two blocks away. Dusk.

Curving, tree-lined streets demarcating small houses that were close, but not touching. A cat racing across a lawn clutched something in its teeth.

"Mrs. Orthway painted her house," Sarah said.

"About time."

"Pretty color."

"Remember when Random was a puppy," Sarah said, "and escaped his baby leash and ran merrily into the street to play and I rushed out after him holding my hand up in the halt position to stop traffic as if I were a policeman?"

A small boy crossed the street in front of them.

"Is that Jimmy Quattrone?" Michael asked.

"Jimmy Quattrone would be thirteen."

"The blink of an eye," Michael said. "That's how long it will be before I retire. What'll we do?"

"Besides being excellent grandparents to Lisa and Camila's babies."

He stopped in front of the redbrick house, where the driveway was empty. A couple of lights were on in the living room.

"They let the ivy grow on the brick," he said.

"They've put the couch facing the fireplace," she said.

The bushes were shaggy.

From this house they'd raced to the police station where Lisa was being detained for shoplifting.

In this house they'd made love on the living room floor, against the closet in the hallway, and under the kitchen table, trying to reach the bedroom.

"Remember the Thanksgiving when your mother asked my father if he knew any Italian songs?" he asked.

"Your father has a lovely voice. Still, an hour . . ."

Through a second-story window, a lamp threw a pool of light.

"I remember the party when I fell down the stairs and fractured my ankle," she said.

"That was a great party," he said.

"Janice and Edgar met that night," she said.

"You predicted they would have great-looking children."

"Toby's not bad."

From this house they'd driven to D.C. for a parade of Vietnam veterans. The veterans had marched by state, the Mississipipi delegation noticeably sparse.

Michael opened the car door. "Let's check on the dogwoods in back."

"They might see you."

He got out and shut the door. He moved down the flagstone path alongside the house, so she followed, walking on her toes when they neared the house, peering through windows. "The paintings are still lifes."

When he got to the kichen door, Michael grabbed the dooknob and tried to open it, but it was locked, and he rattled it, trying to force it, to no avail. He kept walking, through the rotting wooden gate into the backyard.

He groaned.

She ran to catch up, almost slipping on the mossy patio stones, before she saw the giant, limbless carcass of oak throwing a shadow on the house.

Michael turned and headed toward the car. "We should get plants for our front place.

She ran to catch up. "A ficus would be nice."

"Or palms," he said, opening the car door. "A ficus *could* be nice."

"Or palms," she said.

They turned toward the house as they got into the car.

"The windows stick."

"The roof sucks."

He started the car, and made a U-turn. "I drove out to Great Falls this morning, to the inlet where we met." He put his foot on the accelerator. "Let's go to Avignon Freres."

AVIGNON FRERES NO longer existed, so they went to Pearson's.

The restaurant was small and dark — they asked for a booth — and the tables steel-rimmed, splintered wood, painted brown. The light bled in from the window at the far end.

"I'm sorry," Michael said.

He'd wanted to believe that Camila hadn't lied, that she was okay, that he hadn't screwed up as a father again.

The moisture from his beer soaked through the paper napkin. On the wall an orange and black Toulouse-Lautrec poster.

"Okay, here are the things for you," he said, poking around in a brown paper bag. He extracted a book and handed it to her.

"*Gilead*!" She said.

"That's by that author you like, right?" he asked.

"Yes!" She had the book, of course, but that wasn't the point.

He nosed around in his sack again, pulling out two tickets. "And these."

"Movie tickets?"

He nodded.

"What movie?"

"I don't know. But it's at the Museum of Fine Arts." He looked concerned. "That's good, right?"

"Very good!"

"Now!" he said, reaching into the bag, and pulling out a packet triumphantly.

"M&M's!" she said.

Michael shiny with pride.

"I don't have anything for you," she said.

Someone left the restaurant.

Someone came in.

The events of the day washed over them.

Michael shook his head. "People don't know."

He shook his head again, and leaned forward. "There are people, in this country, who don't know who Ho Chi Minh was."

She nodded, took his hand.

They held on for dear life.

SARAH AND JACOB sat on a small grassy hill at an intersection. Telephone pole, mailbox, stop sign. He was wearing another nondescript shirt.

He looked wonderful.

She would give him Peter's phone number at the foundation, and talk with Cynthia about doing an article for the *Globe*.

She looked across the river. "I'm going to have to stop seeing you."

"I know."

"I was using you."

"I know."

Harder than she thought it would be.

Would he be alright.

Would she be alright.

"I'm sorry," she said.

"Does Michael believe you?" he asked.

"Jury's out."

He handed her some books. "I brought a couple of things I thought might help."

She glanced at *1001 Decorating Tips* and *The 60-Minute Gourmet.*

"Just kidding," he said.

"I'll miss Lennie, too," she said. "I think you should get him the iPod."

"You could be right."

"I spoke with the homeless woman in the park," Sarah said. "She has a Ph.D. in English literature."

He nodded. A driver looked for nonexistent street signs.

"If I weren't perfect," Jacob said, "I'd be pitching a fit right now." He blew wisps of hair away from her eyes.

She felt lightheaded.

"You don't need me," she said.

He was silent.

"That's the beauty of an imaginary friend," he said.

A red-tailed hawk, spreading oversized wings, swooped across the river.

Sarah looked over her shoulder. "When I was a child, I had a vision of how I wanted to die. Lying on a bed, holding hands with someone I love, also on the bed, who would die at the same moment and accompany me on the journey."

• • •

SARAH HANDED RACHEL a wrinkled paper bag. "The change-of-address cards you asked for."

The yellow hospice room was plain, but cozy, and silver and pink HAPPY BIRTHDAY letters were strung across the window. It smelled like someone was cooking brussels sprouts.

Rachel took the package. "There's an empty room down the hall that would make a great conference room." She lifted her head and whispered. "A man next door has been here a year.' The doctors keep providing documentation about the precariousness of his health, but here he is!" She sank back into the pillow, her breathing labored. "I'm glad you put your cross back on. Does Michael believe you about Jacob?"

It was hard to hear above Michael's father's singing.

Random napped on the bed, resting his head on Rachel's ankle. A bonsai tree on the bedside table.

"Camila and I are going to see *Control Room* later," Lisa said, wearing a belted, chartreuse tunic over navy blue tights and white boots sprouting gray feathers.

"The ballet's coming next week," Sarah's mother said.

Camila had offered to take Sarah shopping; she'd seen a suit that would look smashing. Michael watched Camila, who remained an enigma.

Last night he'd found the back of Sarah's neck.

"Here, hon" his mother said. "Have some cake." Roses spilling over chocolate.

A teddy bear lounged on a shelf.

Sarah felt something in her pocket; she'd forgotten to return Jacob's key.

"Let me know when it's time for the toasts," Sarah's father said, straightening his tie. "I've prepared some remarks."

Rachel's brother sat in a corner wearing a purple and pink birthday hat, the kind with the rubber strap that hurts your chin, while his daughter played hearts on the floor with Rachel's college roommate, and Rachel's assistant poured red punch into tiny paper cups with orange jack-o'-lanterns on them.

A pile of unopened gifts communed on a table, the Gary Larsen calendar Rachel had requested dressed in cow wrapping paper.

"Next month, Dad and Sarah are going to London," Lisa said to Camila. "Together!"

"Come here," Rachel said to Sarah, her voice faint.

Sarah leaned over the bed, the flowered sheets from Rachel's home, blue blossoms with baby's breath.

"Promise me something," Rachel said, resting between words. "Don't write a sad book."

"But the world — "

"Needs laughter," Rachel said.

"Finiculi, Finicula!"

Rachel looked at Michael's father, then back at Sarah. "Why don't you put on that John Prine song I like?"

Sarah crossed the room to the CD player and slipped

in the disc. Outside the window two small girls played hopscotch, as pink streaks tore across darkening skies.

Sarah whirled around.

Rachel motioned to her assistant, who pulled a wooden chair up to the bed and began making notes on a spiral tablet, per Rachel's instructions, and a nurse wearing a New England Patriots jacket over her white uniform laughed with Delores.

Michael put a hand on Sarah's shoulder, drawing her toward the only unoccupied chair, and she sat on his lap as Prince sang

... build you a home ...

Lisa and Camila danced with Michael's father, Lisa more stiffly than Camila, as Rachel mouthed the words.

... try and find Jesus
on your own ...

MICHAEL TURNED TO SARAH. She leaned in to hear.